Rumors *of* Angels

JOHN VINCENT CONIGLIO

HARVEST HOUSE PUBLISHERS
Eugene, Oregon 97402

RUMORS OF ANGELS

Copyright © 1994 by John Vincent Coniglio
Published by Harvest House Publishers
Eugene, Oregon 97402

Library of Congress Cataloging-in-Publication Data

Coniglio, John Vincent, 1963–
   Rumors of angels / John Vincent Coniglio.
     p. cm.
   ISBN 1-56507-171-9
   1. Prayer in the public schools—Law and legislation—
United States—Fiction. 2. Church and state—United States—
Fiction. 3. Lawyers—United States—Fiction. I. Title.
PS3553.04885R86 1994
813'.54—dc20   93-41096
                                                  CIP

94 95 96 97 98 99 00 — 10 9 8 7 6 5 4 3 2 1

For my mother and father,
who kept the creative fire alive...

Contents

Prologue

A thin curl of smoke was all that greeted attorney Robert Lapper as he cautiously stepped into the penthouse office of the man many considered to be the world's greatest legal mind. The smoke rose above the backside of a tall black leather chair positioned behind a rich mahogany desk that looked more to him like an aircraft carrier than a desk. He heard a soft creak behind him and turned around just quick enough to catch a fleeting glimpse of the receptionist closing the door to the office, leaving him alone in the room. He stood just inside the doorway for a moment with a plastered smile on his face, waiting for the high-backed chair to swivel forward and face him, but the moment passed and the chair did not move. He tapped his foot soundlessly on the plush carpet with his eyes riveted on the chair, prepared for the slightest of movements, but he detected none.

Bob Lapper frowned and thought first about announcing his presence to the inattentive occupier of the chair, but he stopped himself, thinking it might be more appropriate to ask the receptionist to come back in and announce his presence for him. His next thought was to turn tail and get out of there.

After all, he thought to himself, what was he doing here, anyway? He knew he had no place among the ranks of high-powered legal counselors who occupied the top ten floors of this prestigious North Michigan Avenue skyscraper. He was but a lackey, a small-timer, a bumbler who had spent the last fifteen years talking people into coming to his office for consultation, overbilling them for his time, and once in a while, once in a great while, he would find someone ignorant enough to retain him as legal counsel in a case.

He had one now. A case, that was. And he really didn't know why he had been summoned here to meet one of the founding partners of this megafirm. He had work to do back at his office preparing the case he had just gotten, his first real case in years.

This realization angered him slightly, giving him a brief window of confidence that he thought he had better take advantage of before it vanished. Certainly the famous occupier of the chair had heard the receptionist let him in?

Bob Lapper walked forward, determined to get the attention of his disregarding host. But when he realized the back wall of the office he was looking at was not a wall at all, but a window with no visible supports, fifteen feet high and running the entire length of the room, he hesitated. From his vantage point near the doorway, the large mahogany desk appeared to be transposed into the strip of multi-leveled buildings outside the windows. The desk seemed to teeter precariously on the edge of one of the buildings with a far corner floating out mysteriously into a dark blue strip of the evening sky, which perfectly matched the color of the office carpeting. The pointed gothic spires of the *Chicago Tribune* building jutted threateningly through the center of the strange, surrealistic scene, the tallest spire ending exactly where the window met the ceiling. To add to the effect, the cold, crisp air of the late February sky blended the colors of the evening, making a smooth imperceptible transition from the brilliant oranges and reds on the horizon line to the muted purples and pinks of the atmosphere-deflected light to the blues and black of impending night.

He thought again about making a quick exit, and very seriously this time. He had, however, nearly reached one of the visitors' chairs situated in front of the desk, and decided it would be easier just to sit down.

As he sat in the chair, Lapper's eyes were transfixed on the building thunderhead of smoke which seethed its way over him. It was the only other movement in the room aside from his nervous fidgeting.

After a moment, he thought about the peculiar shortness of the chair in which he now sat. He was not a tall man by any standards, yet his knees were at more than right angles to the floor. He placed his briefcase across his knees and it quickly slid into his chest.

This was getting absurd, he thought, and cleared his throat loudly.

Still nothing.

Just then, years of practiced passivity took hold of him. In his day, he had sat idly through much more demanding moments that had commanded action on his part. Besides, a man as important as Will Adam Dysley, of the firm of Dysley, Weber, & Associates, the only law firm to attain a ranking in the Fortune 500, must be doing something of a pressing nature behind the high-backed chair, although he couldn't imagine what.

Lapper looked down at the briefcase that lay wedged between his knees and his chest and noticed a new scuff mark on the corner, as well as a never-before-seen tear in the imitation leather on top. He wondered, quietly to himself, if his being called into this meeting might change the present course of deterioration in his lawyerly apparel.

He was shocked out of his thoughts by a severe rattle of the huge panes of glass along the back wall. The thick panes shook in their tracks as what Lapper surmised to be a strong whirlblast of wind whistled around the upper floors of the building. Just then, with his attention on the windows, he heard the faint creak of the high-backed chair as it began to turn. His eyes darted to the movement and he gulped in a nervous breath. The billowing cloud of smoke trailed the swiveling chair like a great cape.

What faced Bob Lapper was a distinguished-looking, gray-haired man with deep-set, perspicacious eyes whose penetrating gaze immediately served to evaporate the saliva at the back of his throat. He swallowed hard trying to recover the moisture he knew would be necessary to speak, but discovered that it had already found its way down to his hands where it saw fit to pour out of his palms.

The famous counselor wore a finely tailored dark suit with a conservative but not altogether boring tie. His face was cocked in an attempt at a friendly smile, but the pipe smoldering in the corner of his mouth dispelled any hope that it was the least bit genuine.

"Welcome, Bob," said the occupier of the chair, standing and shoving a strong hand out to his guest. "I," he said roughly and removed the pipe from between his teeth, "am Will Dysley."

Lapper thought for a second that he heard the faint sounds of sabers rattling in the distance. "Hello," he said, with an intimidated warble in his voice. Forgetting about his briefcase on his lap, he tried to stand and just barely caught the briefcase as it slid toward a disastrous spill. He got hold of the handle and managed to swing it down to the floor, but not without it clanging against both of his knees. He pushed himself up awkwardly from the low chair. "I'm Bob . . . well, Robert Lapper." He reached out timidly.

"Why, yes, of course," returned Dysley, locking hands with him. "I know," he said, eyeing him with spurious respect. "I know who you are."

Bob Lapper looked back at him in complete surprise.

"Oh, yes," Dysley nodded, reading the disbelief in Lapper's expression. "I've been watching you, Bob."

The famous orator sat back down in his chair. Bob Lapper followed suit, plopping back down awkwardly into the short chair. He sidled in the chair trying to get comfortable, all the time trying to appear poised. He wanted to take Dysley's compliment in stride, but he just couldn't. It was to him so off the wall, bearing in mind his very short list of accomplishments as an attorney, that he simply had to ask.

"Me?" he asked. "You're sure you have been watching the right guy?"

"Yes, Bob, completely," Will said with unswerving confidence.

Lapper smiled giddily and looked satisfied for a moment. But then doubt crept its way back into his head.

"What exactly," he said curiously, "have you been watching me do?"

Will Dysley reached for a finely crafted wooden box on the corner of his desk. He flipped open the box and dug two fingers into the unseen contents. His fingers emerged with a clump of fresh tobacco, which he then inserted into his pipe.

"Let's get right to the point, shall we, Bob," he said condescendingly while reaching into his breast pocket for a book of matches. "My firm has had its eyes on you for the past couple of months and we are very interested in your work. We've had an opening for quite some time at our associates' table in the boardroom, and we feel that you're the best man to fill that seat, Bob."

Will Dysley reached into the top drawer and flipped a lengthy contract onto the desk.

Lapper blinked hard at the name in bold letters on the top page of the document, which was, shockingly enough, his own name. His eyes slowly began to lose clarity as he stared at the page, the first thin clouds of daydream flitting wistfully across his mind.

Dysley sat back in his chair and packed the fresh tobacco firmly in the bowl of his pipe with his thumb. He stuck the pipe back in the corner of his mouth.

"Now, Bob," he said, looking down at Lapper, who snapped to a sort of glazed attention at the mention of his name, "I am prepared to offer you that associate position in the firm, including salary, perks, and bonuses; the secretary in the lobby can give you the rundown of the specifics, since they are, as you might imagine, quite extensive..."

As Dysley spoke, his words gradually lost their individuality to Lapper's preoccupied senses and bled away into an incoherent menagerie of sounds. Lapper found himself following the movements of Dysley's fingers as they tore a match in what appeared to be slow motion from the matchbook and struck it into flame on the back cover. He turned his head to one side like a mesmerized dog as Dysley held the flame over the freshly packed bowl of tobacco. The strands of brown tobacco curled away from the hot flame, and ignited into hot orange. He watched as Dysley wrapped his thin lips around the stem of the pipe. The smooth, bottom arc of the flame was altered as he drew in a breath, the blue-orange heat cascading down into the bowl like a plunging waterfall. The entire bowl glowed with a phosphorescent orange, illuminating Dysley's hard-lined face in the dim light of the late winter evening.

He couldn't have been sure how much was said or how much time had passed while he was lost in a daydream world where he and his wife exchanged friendly nods with congressmen, city officials, and judges and their wives at one of the firm's posh political functions that he had read so much about in the newspapers. All he could be sure of was that his abilities in the realm of legal counseling in no way merited the honor of being a part of this highly reputed law firm. But why not go with the flow, he rationalized inside his head.

Dysley released a long exhale of smoke out of the corner of his mouth, a portion of which wafted directly into Lapper's face. He let out a short cough, which served to partially awaken him from his imaginary wanderings just in time for him to hear, "...it's all yours, Bob, but I must have your answer immediately. Your active files must be transferred to my firm's log as soon as possible."

"I'm sorry?" said Lapper, only now fully returning to reality.

Dysley forced his lips into a smile again. The smoke lingering in his mouth fumed through the crevices of his teeth. "I'll need all your active files to be turned over to my firm immediately," he said with unmistakable clarity. He maintained eye contact with Lapper as long as was necessary to be certain that he understood.

Bob Lapper allowed a childish grin to surface. *An associate position,* he thought, *at Dysley, Weber, & Associates? This was too much! Wait until I tell my wife! But why me? And what about this man seated across from me? Can I trust him after seeing what the media has said about what a manipulative man Will Dysley is?*

And then, smack dab in the middle of second-guessing his luck, it happened. When it was he himself who was the benefactor of Dysley's manipulation, all that Bob Lapper had read about the ruthless, conniving man before him burned away like the morning dew. All that remained were unequivocal opportunities for personal gain and a faint mist of rumored accusations and unfounded allegations against a wholly innocent and...well, quite noble man. Suddenly his private practice in the stinky little executive suite on the south side with the day-old doughnuts in the lobby didn't look so good. He now found his allegiance firmly aligned with the man puffing away on his pipe behind the desk.

"Of course," Lapper laughed, "I'll have to confer with my client, I mean *clients,*" he corrected, chuckling awkwardly, trying not to give away the sad truth of his single-entry case log, "to see if they have any objections. I mean, I can't see how they would. Look at what they're getting." Lapper careened his head around at the surrounding office. "Definitely a trade up, wouldn't you say, Mr. Dysley?"

"My secretary will handle the signing of the contract, Bob," Dysley said, motioning to the door and handing him the papers. "She will also take care of the legal transfer of your active files to the firm's log."

Dysley rose from his chair and held out a firm hand. "Let me be the first to congratulate you, Bob, as the newest associate at Dysley, Weber, and Associates."

Lapper stood and grasped Dysley's hand, still sporting his childish grin.

After years of ill-fortune compounded with bad breaks, it appeared that by some stroke of incredible luck, Bob Lapper's meager lifestyle was about to change. He was now, amazingly, a part of the highest-grossing law firm in the country—one of the few entrusted associates who were allowed to work side by side with perhaps history's greatest legal mind. And he hadn't the faintest idea why.

Dumbfounded by what had just transpired, the small-time attorney slowly backed his way to the door, clutching his dilapidated briefcase hard to his chest. He watched as the famous counselor sat back into his plush leather chair and swiveled around to face the Chicago skyline now completely engulfed by the night. Another fierce gust of late-winter wind gushing down from the north shook the huge panes of glass. He stayed just long enough to see a fresh curl of smoke rise from behind the high-backed chair.

1

Planting the Seed

"NO DISRESPECT, Professor... er, *your Honor,*" the young student corrected himself while striding along a row of twelve fellow students who were sitting in folding chairs at the front of a large classroom, "but I just don't see it being so cut-and-dried. It's not that I deny their learned wisdom on the subject," he continued, "it's more that I question *how* they learned it and *where* they learned it from."

The law professor, adorned in full parliamentary dress right down to the eighteenth-century wig and robe, looked puzzlingly over at his student.

"Our Constitution specifies certain constraints on society," the young student continued, "yet the minds which determined those constraints were shaped by an entirely different set of experiences and circumstances than those which face us today. For example, as children, none of us were subjected to the heretical doctrines of the Church of England, a powerful governing body which essentially ruled the land. My church governed about an hour of my time on Sunday mornings, and even that was negotiable if there was a good game on the tube!"

A smattering of laughter trickled across the student assembly.

"I for one," continued the counsel for the defense, "simply fail to see the relevance of the graduation prayer in question to the constitutional law prohibiting Congress from establishing a universal religion. There seems to be no apparent danger of a universal religion being established if we permit this harmless little prayer to be read at the ceremony. And certainly the prayer in question presents no threat whatsoever to the status quo of our society."

"Amen, brother!" shouted a sarcastic voice from the back of the classroom. The assembly erupted in laughter. The attorney for the defense was not amused.

"And I submit!" yelled the determined student above the roaring laughter. "Had the founding fathers of the United States been writing in the present instead of two hundred years ago, and given the current state of affairs in our country, I believe they would have delineated our religious freedoms more clearly."

He continued to pace around the twelve students who comprised the jury. "I am not denying that these were great men," he said shaking his head, "but I refuse to admit that they were omniscient. I refuse to accept that they were able to see into the future and anticipate changes in society and the ridiculous degree to which people would carry the interpretation of their original words. They were, after all, men—not prophets!"

University of Chicago Law School student Randell Clive took his seat at the table for the defense.

The professor pushed back his chair abruptly and walked over to the blackboard, his robe flowing behind him. The taps and swishes of chalk on chalkboard echoed throughout the otherwise silent assembly. He wrote so vigorously that his whole body shook and the curly parliamentary wig nearly fell off of his head. The students bit their tongues holding in their laughter. They strained their eyes to read what he had scrawled on the board; it was written in the illegible handwriting professors are known for.

It read: UNSUBSTANTIATED RELIGIOUS CLAIMS!!! and was emphasized by a telltale, ornate slash under the words, which was a pretty solid indication that this phrase would appear on an upcoming exam. The students wrote feverishly on their notepads trying to record the phrase, fully expecting the professor to go off on a heartfelt dissertation. In an entire semester it had never failed. After he wrote with that intensity on the chalkboard, he was sure to explode with law commentary certain to appear on a test. If they weren't prepared when he began to rattle off courtroom doctrine, they would be sure to miss something. They sat tensely with poised pens.

"This," said the professor while tapping on the board with the stub of chalk, "has no place in the courtroom, Mr. Clive. Have you read the brief?" The professor stormed over to his table and flipped wildly through the pages of the briefing, the tails of his wig swinging comically from side to side. He stopped on a page, using his finger to scan its contents.

"Here, here it is," he said. "Listen to this, people; listen to what it is really saying." And he read, "We acknowledge our dependence on the resurrected Savior Jesus Christ to guide us in our endeavors in the years ahead. In His name we pray." The professor paused.

"Did you hear that?" he asked in disbelief. "Did you all hear that? For those of you who spent the weekend slammin' liquor instead of slammin' law, that is part of the graduation ceremony prayer in question in this mock trial of ours!"

The professor stormed back over to the blackboard and slashed two more emphasis lines underneath the phrase he had written earlier. On the final exaggerated slash, the stubby piece of chalk broke off and flew out from between his fingers and trickled down the platform, causing his thumbnail to career into the blackboard and make a hideous screech.

"Is this the sort of direction we want our graduates to have?" the professor inquired, looking out over the auditorium of young minds.

"Well, is it?" he asked, leaving the matter open for comment. Most of the students had learned by now to keep quiet when the professor was on one of his rampages. They all sunk down in their chairs, trying to make themselves invisible. Yet there was one student who had the insolence to offer his comment and opinion at times like these. One student who was well-versed enough in the tenets of law to talk shop with the professor even in this, his second year of law school. An exemplary student who happened to be the opposing counsel in the mock trial.

"If I may, your Honor," said that particular brazen student, nodding cordially at the professor and calmly rising from behind the table at the front of the room.

"This year's graduating class," he began, "has invested thousands of dollars learning how to disassociate fact from fantasy, and as a final send-off into the world beyond the sheltered existence of the university, a world of reality, we're offering them *a religious myth as their system of guidance?* I think we must ask ourselves, where is the logic in that?"

The heads of the other students followed the guy who had set the high limit on the bell curve for every exam this semester as he walked slowly in front of the mock jury. They had come to know the potential of his sharp mind very well over the semester. It's not often that you see such a rare mix of arrogance and genius; it sort of makes a person hard to forget.

They noticed that he wore another of the dark suits that, even at this age, must have lined his closets. They saw that his tie was one of many he had that skirted the fine line between being conservative but not altogether boring. They also noticed that he held, as usual, and quite presumptuously for such a young man, a smoking pipe in his hand. Young Randell Clive shook his head as he watched the arrogant student systematically tear through his argument and humiliate him in front of the class as he had humiliated most other students. Clive's anger swelled with each point he made. Even the professor of this course entitled "Practical Application and Hypothetical Cases" did not seem immune to the piercing logic of the young student. He watched and listened as intently as the class.

"And," the confident young man who had acquired the gesticulations of a seasoned attorney continued, "as for the issue of the credibility and longstandingness of the words of our nation's founding fathers, I have but one argument."

He turned to Clive, who looked infuriatingly back at him.

"They've gotten us this far, haven't they?" he said, smiling. "Their Constitution has made us the strongest nation in the world economically, militarily, and most of all, politically. Our founding fathers have given us a *living document* which lends itself to interpretation and which is pliable and adaptable to the future needs of our evolving society. The proof lies in the efficiency of the system they created. A system which, I might add, includes the nation's courts of law."

The young man reached Clive at the table for the defense and calmly sat on the edge and brushed off his pant leg. The professor slowly removed his white wig, being careful not to disturb the eloquent dissertation of his prized student.

"They designed the court system as the proving ground for unsubstantiated claims of any nature, Mr. Clive," the student continued, "including those of a religious nature." He leaned back on his hands, his legs dangling off the edge of the table. "Therefore, Mr. Clive," he proceeded, "I recommend that you make use of a system that has worked without fail for the past two hundred years. If you feel you have a claim or an assumption that has the potential for substantiation, I suggest that you take *it,* the source of the claim, *not some result of it,* through the proper established channels."

The cocky youth reached in his pocket and removed a book of matches and calmly lit one and held it over his pipe. He released several puffs of smoke from the corner of his mouth. It had seemed strange at first to the students that the professor would allow him to smoke in class, but he was a most unusual student, the likes of which the university had never seen before.

"Mr. Clive," the student continued, taking the pipe from his mouth, "I urge you to take your Christian beliefs elsewhere, because as the professor has written, unsubstantiated claims do not belong in a court of law. The prayer in question, as well as prayer in general, is an act stemming from a belief. Prove the belief itself to be rooted in fact, and the prayer stands uncontested," he said simply.

"You see, Mr. Clive, it is not the prayer that needs to be on trial, but the reason there is a prayer in the first place. You need to start where it all began," he said, trying hard to hold back a wicked smile, "with the myth that is the basis for the hope that exists in the prayers of people."

The professor watched the blossoming talent of this student who had a gift far and above anyone he had ever taught in his classroom. He marveled at how the words seemed to flow in such eloquent precision, the conviction with which they were delivered. His curiosity was piqued by the substance of what his student was saying. As far as he knew, this was a unique, although somewhat absurd, approach to the issue of prayer at a public ceremony; that is, if he had correctly guessed the conclusion of genius student Will Dysley.

"It's your Christ that needs to be put on trial," shouted young Will Dysley to his classmate, who grew more bitter by the moment. "Turn Christ's resurrection myth into reality and you won't have to concern yourself with petty arguments involving the founding fathers, the Constitution, and what you believe to be the misapplications of its tenets. You will have proven that the hope we place in Christ through prayer is not unfounded but substantiated by evidence and proof recognized as such by our system of law."

The assembly grew restless as slowly they began to realize where young Dysley was heading. Some were shocked, others smirked and grinned and whispered among themselves, knowing that they were about to see their classmate humiliated.

"Your goal is simple," Dysley raised his voice to be heard above the rustlings of the class. "Simply prove by means accepted in our courts of law that a man named Jesus Christ was indeed resurrected from the tomb and is alive today."

There was a great uproar from the students. Their laughter was loud and unending. The ridicule in Will's voice had been clear.

Randell Clive burned in his mind an impression of the feeling he had at that moment—a feeling that would stick with him for many years to come. The seeds of vengeance took firm hold in the fertile, formative soil of his young mind. He locked eyes with Will Dysley, who sat grinning down at him, mocking him and his potential as a trial lawyer. He looked at him with the contempt of a slave to his master.

"All right, Mr. Dysley," boomed the professor, "I think Mr. Clive has had enough. I think we've all had enough."

The professor placed the fake wig back on top of his head. "We have reached a verdict," he said with the regal tone of a judge. "This year's graduating class in the year of 1967 will be treated to a moment of silence at the graduation ceremony, and not a prayer as per the constraints of the Constitution of the United States as it is interpreted today." He then slammed his gavel, which was really a rubber mallet, onto the table. "Mr. Dysley is the victor," he said. "Case closed."

The students gathered their things preparing to leave.

Randell Clive pushed through the crowd which had rushed to the front of the classroom and stood between him and Will Dysley. He had a look of vengeance in his eyes. Through the crowd, he saw his quarry calmly filling his pipe with a fresh clump of tobacco. After a few more determined twists and turns of his body, he arrived face to face with his ridiculer.

"I do not know the reason you felt the need to so greatly humiliate me," said Clive through clenched teeth, "and at this point I don't really care. What I do want you to know is that one day a case will come along, a case taken from the true battles going on around us in the lives of people. And I will take that case to the highest trial court in the land. It will be a case that will serve to tear down current constitutional constraints and give society the hope it needs in the modern age filled with negativity and despair!"

Will Dysley did not flinch. He let a smile spread slowly across his face.

"Choose your case well, my friend," he said as coldly as the winter wind. "Because you can bet, whatever it takes, I'll be there at the other end to stop you."

For a long moment the two young men stared intensely into one another's eyes, holding their territories like two alpha male wolves. Finally, they turned and left the classroom.

The two law students were not to have another encounter in their remaining years at the University of Chicago Law School. In fact, after the final examination in the course, they were not to see each other for the next twenty-five years.

2

Dysley, Weber, & Associates

FOR WILL DYSLEY, it was a situation he had experienced many times before, only never of this magnitude. Media vans from local and national television stations lined the street in front of the downtown courthouse with huge satellite dishes adorning their roofs, and men and women worked frantically to unload their equipment. Police units had cordoned off access to the courthouse steps from the mass of demonstrators that filled the mall area.

From their seat in the back of the sleek black limousine, Will Dysley and his partner Tom Weber could see the flashing white signs of the protesters. There was unequivocal anger in the few signs that they could read.

One sign in particular struck a chord deep in the financial sensibilities of Tom Weber, *the* Weber in the megafirm of Dysley, Weber, & Associates. The sign read, "Christianity Is a Bad Joke, and Our Children Are the Victims of the Cruel Punchline." He could hold back no more.

"Will," he said hesitantly as he studied the scene outside the darkly tinted windows, "are you sure we want to do this?"

A policeman approached the car as it neared the barricaded area in front of the steps. The driver flashed an access card, and the officer waved them through.

"How did all these people find out about the trial?" asked Weber, clearly disturbed by the scene.

Will Dysley let loose a stream of pipe smoke that quickly exited through a crack in the window on his side of the car. "Challenge a constitutional amendment," he said in a low raspy voice, "and the nation's ears swivel and twitch. Swirl in a hint of sensationalism and you've got a media frenzy."

As if on cue, the limousine came to a stop and was quickly surrounded by anxious members of the press. The driver stepped out, forced his way through the crowd of reporters, and swung open the back door. Dysley and Weber emerged into the cold of the February morning. The air around them quickly filled with steam from the hot breath of the press as they rifled their questions and hopes for comment at the firm representing the defense in the trial set to begin.

A second limousine pulled to a stop behind the lead car and Dysley's infamous *Legal Entourage* smoothly exited, clothed in high-powered suits, toting well-laden briefcases. They all wore navy blue, men and women alike, and mirrored sunglasses that reflected the vivid blue of the morning sky. These were the researchers, the people who dug up the dirt. Not many young attorneys would ever dream of subjecting themselves to being in the employ of "The Man," as the entourage members not-so-affectionately called their monarchical boss when they were more than sure the coast was clear. Weber, they knew, was essentially a subject, like themselves, in Dysley's kingdom.

With practiced ease, Dysley and Weber repulsed the probing questions and evaded the jabbing microphones of the media and hurriedly began their ascent of the stairs. The entourage of sharp legal aids trailed the two prefectural partners at a respectable distance. In this wilderness, deterrent behavioral posturing failed miserably in the crazed irrational faces and gnashing teeth of the jackals that surrounded them. In this wilderness, the only deterrent was speed.

"Let's pick up the pace, people," Dysley shouted sharply over his shoulder. "We've got new law to write!" he screamed, using his favorite pretrial slogan.

Garbled shouts flew from the mass of protesters as the representatives of the powerful law firm bounded up the courthouse steps. From the four corners of the globe they had come to gather and to watch the historic proceedings. Later on, city officials would accurately estimate their ranks at half a million.

Tom Weber, although the younger of the two partners, wheezed as he tried to match Dysley's quickened gait. Even the fine tailoring of his suit and flowing long wool coat couldn't hide his distended stomach and short legs. Climbing these steps, like anything else physical, had always been considered a chore for the less energetic founding partner of the firm.

Weber had always been portly since childhood, and he had added a few inches in recent years, preparing for his goal of a comfortable, quiet retirement. A goal that was, he believed, hopelessly in jeopardy if his partner was to proceed as planned in the trial that awaited them at the top of the steps.

He had puzzled long and hard while lying awake in bed on recent sleepless nights, unable to answer the question which kept popping into his head. Why would a man who had attained just about every plateau in the realm of law want to sink his entire reputation knee-deep into such a controversial trial as this? Dysley had made three appearances before the U.S. Supreme Court, all of which he won handily. He had posted several State Supreme Court victories that had propelled him to fame and a status of indestructibility in his home state of Illinois. All of this had combined to buy him several houses and various other possessions that were fit for royalty.

Again the portly partner could not help but wonder, especially since that reputation being sunk knee-deep into this controversial trial was, disturbingly, half his.

"Will," he wheezed, "for goodness' sake wait up!"

Will paused on a step without turning around, his eyes remaining focused on the doorway at the top of the steps.

"And, well," said Weber, breathing heavily as he finally reached the step where Dysley waited, "I guess that's precisely it. I mean, our Christian account base. We can kiss them good-bye if you don't change your tune." Tom licked his dry lips.

"Tom," said Will, still peering up at the top of the steps, "you're doing it again." He smiled and shook his head.

"I'm about to begin a trial here," he continued. "I haven't the time for your doomsaying; what I need now is your support, partner." Will turned around to see his partner of over twenty years hunched over with his hands resting on his knees as he panted noisily. In the cold winter air, whitish-gray steam billowed from Tom's nostrils like breath from a hostile bull. "Stand up, Tom," he said and grabbed his arm. "Stand up and take a look back there."

Tom Weber slowly pushed himself up and looked back over his shoulder. As far as he could see, the demonstrators were packed into the courthouse mall area. The horde of thousands swayed and undulated, varying the patterns of multitudinous colors. Their white protest signs bobbed and waved and flashed like reflected sunlight on a roiling sea.

"Dysley, Weber, & Associates was founded with the objective of changing the world," Will spouted regally. "Through the years, our names have come to be associated with trials like this that challenge the accepted structure of society."

Will took a deep breath and scanned the horizon line of protesters. He stretched out his chin and clenched his jaw tightly. "This is the big one I've been dreaming about, partner," he said, nodding satisfactorily. "This is the one that will ensure our place in the history books," he said, then turned to continue his ascent of the steps. Weber got a hold of his arm and stopped him.

"It's not too late to turn back, Will," he said, still somewhat out of breath and dabbing his forehead with his handkerchief. "We can talk with counsel for the plaintiff and have him join with us in a motion to set aside the special Supreme Court dispensation, fall back on the Constitution and the Establishment Clause. Put this thing where it should be; there's no reason for such a controversial approach to this issue."

Will turned again to face his partner.

"We did not bring this action before the court," said Will, staring down at his arm, which Weber still held, "the plaintiff did. He is the one who got his unique approach to this well-tried issue approved, and I'm certainly not going to let this opportunity pass me by. I've waited too long for this, Tom, and this great nation is more than ready for this issue to come to trial."

"Ah, Will!" exploded Tom, throwing up his arms in frustration. "Maybe we can talk the plaintiff into a dismissal or something! There must be some way to stop this madness!"

Will looked disappointingly at Tom.

"I'm not looking for some hollow victory here, Tom," he said evenly, "some easy concession of defeat. You should know that is not the way I operate. I'm out for blood, friend, as usual." Will pulled his arm away and bounded up the few remaining steps.

Tom looked dejectedly down at the cement. "I can still hope, can't I?" he said meekly to himself.

The fast-moving *Legal Entourage* bumped by him like a passing freight train on their way up the steps. Tom could envision the firm's account base dwindling before his eyes. He shook his head, trying to determine the source of his partner's obsession with this particular case. *Why rock the boat in the twilight of such a brilliant career?* In twenty years of association with this man he had never seen him this way. *What was it about this case?* he thought.

Will Dysley stood for a moment at the top of the steps and gazed back over the swirling throngs of demonstrators, media personnel, and police crowd-control units. He narrowed his eyes into a biting blast of cold wind off frozen Lake Michigan as he scanned the courthouse mall area from horizon to horizon. Dysley filled his lungs with the revitalizing freshness of the northern air, his disciplined mind acutely aware of the crosscurrents of sentiment rising from the crowd before him. *This,* he thought, raising an eyebrow, *is exactly what I want to cap my distinguished career. As well as the perfect opportunity to say hello to an old friend.*

Deep in his subconscious, however, there was another reason why he had to go through with the trial. So deep in fact that even the man who considered himself the most perceptive trial attorney in the world did not know of its existence.

3

Venire Facias de Novo

RANDELL CLIVE turned around a little nervously at his table. He had heard of the last-minute change in the law firm handling the defense in the case and he was anxious to catch the first glimpse of his old adversary.

Clive had retained much of his youthful looks over the years and added very little to his law school weight. He was tall and thin and sported a well-pressed olive-colored suit with a stylishly matched olive pin-striped shirt and floral silk tie. He had added knowledge, however, since those days of his youth, and experience that shone clearly through his dark, tilted eyes. His skin was pale and tight over the bony contours of his face, further accentuating the darkness of his eyes, and his hair was closely cropped along the sides with a tuft of curl on top.

Alongside him at the table was the most beautiful

little girl, and next to her was her mother. Turning back around, Clive was faced with the ear-to-ear smile of the little girl, who gazed up at him with stunningly large, clear blue eyes. He looked first at the blond-haired little girl, who wore a frilly white dress, and then at her mother, who was a model match to the young girl only in adult proportions. Their warm smiles served to abate the rise in nervousness that he was feeling, replacing it with a smile of his own.

He had waited a long time for little Mary Magellan to come walking into his life, although he had not, in the least, left it up to random chance. An indelible memory and a damaged psyche had driven him to do everything he could to locate a case like Mary's—a case that was right up his alley.

Two years out of law school, Clive had started his own Chicago-based firm, specializing in cases which challenged the Supreme Court's interpretations of what they and enlightened people everywhere deemed to be the intent of the original words of the U.S. Constitution. His firm had received national attention on several occasions, winning some victories—albeit minor—in altering current constitutional constraints placed upon people, but a case with the potential for that major triumph he had dreamed about still eluded him...until now.

One of the staff members at Clive's law firm was responsible for perusing the pages of small hometown newspapers across the country, especially the religious sections, to look for anything that could be even remotely connected to the fulfillment of an old promise some twenty-five years in the making. It was a blurb in the *Glengrove Gazette,* the local newspaper for the small town of Glengrove, Illinois—a suburb on the south side of Chicago—that offered the opportunity to make it a promise twenty-five years in the keeping.

Randell Clive, the blood of vengeance surging through his veins, did not waste any time contacting the mother of the little girl he had read about in the *Gazette.* It had not been easy to convince Elizabeth Magellan, Mary's mother, to proceed with the case; she did not want to subject her little girl to the rigors of a trial; she was worried that it might have some lasting effect on her future. Yet he talked to her about the importance of the case for us all, and finally, after a couple of weeks, Elizabeth relented and the promise Clive had made so long ago in law school was given its birth in the trial court system.

Randell Clive vowed to avenge the humiliation suffered in his youth. What he did not know, however, was that the very progenitor of that humiliation, the man who had planted the seed, would also hold fast to his promise made in a death-locked stare in the classroom of their youth, and would soon be sitting across the aisle from him.

Just then, Clive heard a ruckus behind him. He turned around to see if it was what he thought it was. Little Mary and her mother Elizabeth followed his lead, looking over their shoulders in unison at the door of the courtroom. What Clive saw confirmed that the media reports had been correct.

Will Dysley, like a solitary warrior, always entered the courtroom alone.

A recent article hyping the trial had told of this little tidbit of strategy used by the world-famous counselor. Clive recalled a quote from Dysley in the article stating that when he entered the courtroom with his *Legal Entourage* in tow, Dysley felt that his "overwhelming presence" and the discomfort it caused to the opposing counsel was in danger of being dissevered from its mark.

It was true that Dysley's opponents seldom escaped at least slight feelings of discomfort in the knowledge of what awaited them at the thorny tip of the tongue of the seasoned jurisprudent. More than a few witnesses, opposing counselors, and jurists—and in one case, a judge—had fallen prey to the master orator's ability to find the flaw in their testimony or argument. Regardless of its size or emotional impact on the individual, the flaw was then enlarged to become integral to the validity of the testimony or the argument, and systematically dismantled until there was no longer any structure, no longer any foundation, and finally, no longer any case.

Will Dysley walked the length of the center aisle from the courtroom doors to the counselors' tables entirely by himself. Randell Clive, his client, and her mother watched as he neared their table.

Behind him in the doorway, Clive thought he caught a glimpse of one of the members of Dysley's *Legal Entourage* peering around the edge of the door but then quickly pulling back. Clive wondered at what point the entourage was free to follow their boss into the courtroom. Did it have something to do with the number of steps he took, or an imaginary line across a certain point in the courtroom? Or, perhaps it had something to do with what happened next.

It is incredible how eye contact with someone you haven't seen in twenty-five years can make you feel the exact same way you felt the last time you had eye contact with that person. Clive felt a sensation that was somewhat familiar, like that of being a naive student again. He was not sure if it was the resurfacing of the academic inferiority he had felt in that classroom so many years ago, or if Dysley did indeed possess some type of power to intimidate his opponents, forcing them back to a time of uncertainty from their past.

All he knew was that when his old classmate locked eyes with him as he passed by, he felt like a lump of moistened clay ready for shaping. He felt himself being transported back to a state of unclarity; he began to doubt his abilities, to flip-flop synapses in his mind, trading those well-stocked memory chips containing knowledge accumulated through years of experience for chips garbled in misperceptions and immature imaginings. If it had not been for the soft, angelic voice of Mary Magellan, Clive's metagenesis may have continued, rendering him unable to present his opening argument effectively.

"Who's that man?" she asked and playfully fluffed her dress. "And why is he looking at you that way?" she frowned.

Randell Clive shook himself loose from the grip that held him and his mind regained, in an instant, its perception of reality. He thought he could almost hear the faint whir of the generator that turned the turbines in his mind. The whirring noise, it turned out, was the media personnel at the back of the courtroom testing their cameras to make sure they were in order before the trial started. Nevertheless, he definitely felt more like a man ready to fulfill a long-sought-after dream than he did a moistened lump of clay ready for shaping.

"Honey," said Elizabeth, grasping her daughter gently by the wrist, "Mr. Clive has things to do. No more questions for now."

"No, it's all right, Miss Magellan," said Clive brightly. He leaned toward Mary and tapped the tip of her nose gently with his finger. "After all, it is her trial."

"And my time in the detention room," Mary said, giggling.

Elizabeth gave her daughter an unamicable stare. Mary's smile quickly flipped to a frown and she averted her eyes toward the floor.

"That man," said Clive, nodding over at Will Dysley, who was taking his place at the table across the aisle, "to answer your question, Mary, is the reason we are here today."

The courtroom continued to fill with people.

The room itself was stupendous. Wide, dark wooden beams ran horizontally along the length of the ceiling. Heavy wooden support pilasters rose from the floor. Diffused sunlight cascaded in through the huge rectangular stained-glass windows along the sides of the room, bathing the court in an almost unnatural light.

Red and gold tapestry that looked either dusty or extremely old hung in three loops between the beams directly over the judge's chair, which was the centerpiece of the courtroom, both literally and figuratively.

The trunk-like mahogany base of the judge's podium appeared larger-than-life rising up, as it did, to such a height. There were fine relief carvings on the base depicting scenes from Egypt and the pyramids of the pharaohs. Sitting high at the top was the judge's stake-backed chair with arm pads the color of dried blood—as if blood had been smeared there from the palms of the chair's occupant and left to dry.

Media personnel scuttled along the floor twisting and securing the cables for their equipment. Lighting people took readings in front of the jury box, at the counselors' tables, at the witness stand, and, standing on a ladder, at the judge's chair.

The judge had allowed the cameras to be placed in the courtroom, one in each corner, due to the highly relevant nature of the arguments to be presented in the trial to the lives of the millions of TV viewers at home. The cameras sat unyieldingly on tripods, their rapacious corneas preparing to dictate not only what the world was to see of the trial, but at what particular angle they were to see it.

Even the bailiff was caught up in the media fever and made certain to put his best side toward the closest camera before he spoke.

"All rise!" he yelled above the chatter of the crowded courtroom. "The honorable Judge Montgomery Alexander presiding!"

It is hard for a man to move as slowly and decrepitly as Judge Alexander did while still retaining his dignity. He had the face of a man you wanted to respect, no matter how antiestablishment you were. He was short and thin, and had a narrow strip of what remained of his hair along the back of his head. His eyes were deep set and, it appeared, full of wisdom—the kind of eyes that saw everything even if they weren't necessarily where the everything was taking place.

The courtroom crowd quieted down and stood at attention, waiting for the judge's cue to let them take their seats. The old man nodded ever so slightly before he slid slowly into his chair and assumed a position that appeared so comfortable, it was as if he had slipped into a prefabricated mold. He carefully placed his bifocals into a crevice low on his nose and began to leaf through the papers in front of him.

"Ahhumm," his voice warbled as he cleared his throat. "What do we have here," he half-muttered to himself. "Magellan versus Longview Elementary." He nonchalantly shuffled a few papers and looked down his nose at them.

"I have something here I need to read for..." Judge Alexander peered suspiciously over his glasses at the flashing red lights on top of the cameras that recorded his every move, "...for all of you," he finished sarcastically.

"For those of you who do not know," the judge continued in a voice far more commanding than he had used thus far, "a jury is not usually necessary in cases involving interpretation of the Constitution.

"The intricacies of the words and phrases contained in the Constitution has, previously, been left up to the assessments of those educated in the rhetoric and ideology of that document. This case is different. The opinion handed to me from the Supreme Court of the United States is this:

> *Due to the unique nature of the argumental approach chosen by the counsel for the plaintiff in the case of Magellan versus Longview Elementary, an approach hereby accepted and approved for trial by this court, and due to the fact that the decision lies not in the interpretation of the doctrine of the Constitution, but in an area far removed from such; an area of interpretation warranting the judgmental abilities of common people, we the Supreme Court of the land order venire facias de novo.*

The judge removed his bifocals.

"What that all means," he said matter-of-factly, "is that we're going to have a jury."

As if on cue, a door creaked open behind the jury box, and the bailiff escorted twelve men and women into the courtroom. They sat in seats in the order they entered, in two rows of six each.

"Now then," said the judge, "now that *we're all here*," he added invectively, "perhaps we can begin. Mr. Clive, you have the floor for your opening argument."

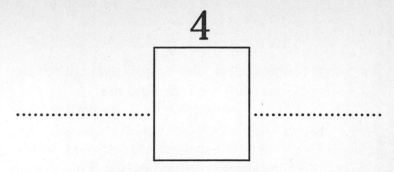

4

Forbidden Ground

RANDELL CLIVE had waited a long time for the introduction he had just heard. He thought it would be hard to control the elation he was sure would well up inside of him when he heard it. He thought that it would definitely be the happiest moment of his lawyerly career.

He couldn't have been more wrong.

It wasn't nervousness or fear that he was feeling, he thought to himself as the judge's words reached him. It wasn't regret. It was more like the feeling someone might have as he tries to swim the Atlantic Ocean, gets halfway across, and decides he had better go back. To Randell Clive, Judge Alexander's words meant simply that now there was no turning back. He knew that he was embarking onto untrodden ground, legally speaking, and that in the minds of some of the protesters outside the courthouse, it was more like *forbidden* ground.

He stood rather hesitantly at first, but then his seasoned lawyerly instincts took over. He walked to the center of the floor with renewed authority and dedication to the realization of a dream twenty-five years in the making. His longtime enemy observed his every move from the table for the defense, the judge and jury anxiously sidled in their chairs awaiting his long-awaited, much-anticipated opening argument, and the entire world made a last dash to the fridge before returning to their living rooms to watch what promised to be riveting courtroom drama.

"Thank you, your Honor," counselor Clive began, his arms folded pensively across his chest. He freed up a hand to caress the contours of his chin.

"On September 4, 1990," he said staring down at the floor, "at approximately 7:30 A.M. a small, solitary figure stood at the flagpole of Longview Elementary School in Glengrove, a suburb south of our city."

Clive unfolded his arms, squatted down, and drew an imaginary circle on the floor. The media tech crews, viewing the action from their remote location in the studios, wished they had taken the time to mount a sky cam on the ceiling. But who could've known?

"Around the solitary figure," he illustrated, "school buses dropped off their loads of subdued youngsters, who clustered on the playground savoring their last precious few minutes of freedom. The kids were subdued because this was the first day of school, summer was over, and there would be new lockers to find, new teachers to meet.

"But the solitary figure remained standing by the flagpole," he said pointing at the center of his imaginary circle while looking up at the jurists.

"However, the silent vigil of the small figure," he continued, "did not go unnoticed. The teacher on playground duty went to the figure to investigate. As the teacher approached, she realized that the figure was a little girl standing for no apparent reason next to the flagpole." Clive pointed again at the center of his imaginary circle.

"As she got even closer, it became clear what the little girl was doing. She saw that the girl's eyes were closed, and that her hands . . ." Clive paused and raised his hands while looking directly at the jurists ". . . were folded together," he finished.

He slowly brought his own hands together, closed his eyes, and dropped to his knees. He let the image of himself kneeling in the middle of the courtroom sink into the minds of the judge and jury. In mere seconds, he would prey upon that image and the emotions it elicited.

"It quickly became obvious to the teacher that the little girl was *praying*," he said suddenly, snapping his eyes open and pulling his hands apart as if he had been scorched by a searing flame.

Randell Clive pushed himself to his feet and brushed the dust off his knees. He walked over to the jury box and leaned against the wooden railing.

"You see," he continued, "a network of churches across the state of Illinois had set this date, September 4, and this time, 7:30 A.M., and this location, the school flagpole, for our children to gather. The churches called it "I'll Meet You at the Pole," and it was for schoolchildren at every grade school, teens at every high school, and students at every college in the state.

"The purpose of this gathering," Clive said while turning to face the audience assembled in the courtroom, "was not for tryouts for a team, or for practice, or to organize a pep rally. This gathering was for children with another agenda, another interest.

"Across the state, our children came to the flagpole for a single unified purpose," Clive said, holding up a strong finger.

"They came," he stated with deep significance, "to spend a moment with Jesus."

Behind him the media people scribbled wildly on their notepads and camera crews rechecked their cameras to make sure they were getting all this on tape. Things had better be right, or they wouldn't have a job in the afternoon. To miss this was like falling asleep the minute before the once-in-a-lifetime appearance of Halley's Comet fireballing its way across the heavens. There just was no next time.

History, it is said, cannot wait for technical difficulties.

"According to the statistics of the churches that organized the event," said Clive as he walked toward the courtroom audience, "forty thousand students from the very young to the old met that morning at flagpoles across the state.

"At Longview Elementary School, however, the turnout was not so great."

Clive had arrived at the table where his clients sat. He sat on the edge of the table and focused his gaze on the beautiful mother/daughter team, causing everyone to look at them, including the camera in the front-left corner of the courtroom, which quickly switched to tele-photo for a close-up.

"At Longview Elementary," he said with a warm smile, "there was only Mary."

Mary's eyes widened at the mention of her name. She buried her head into her mother's shoulder. Elizabeth put her arm around her daughter and snugged her close.

"A harmless event, you might say. An innocent mo-ment spent by the flagpole? Hardly!" Clive boomed. "Not at Mary's school and, it turns out, not at any of our children's schools. You see, little Mary was quickly whisked into the principal's office." Mary nuzzled her head even further into the protective shielding of her mother's side. The folks at home got a great close-up shot of a frightened little girl.

"The principal remembered Mary; she had been in his office last year. Yes, he remembered; Mary was a repeat offender. This, said the principal to little Mary, is your second offense, and he asked her if she planned to pray at school again.

"Mary's innocent answer was, simply, yes. The prin-cipal promptly called Miss Magellan and threatened to expel Mary if she were caught praying again.

"Harsh stuff, it seems, for a little silent prayer at a flagpole," Clive said with disbelief, "but entirely within the law as it stands today. A law straight out of the Constitution as it is currently interpreted.

"You see, in our schools," he explained, standing up from his position on the table, "the act of praying or acts associated with prayer are considered crimes—the same as chewing gum during class, or passing notes, or smoking in the bathroom. All of these offenses will get you time in detention or expulsion from school, depending on the severity." He made his way back to the jury box.

"Why do you think it is a crime to pray in school?" he said inquisitively to the jurists and all present in the courtroom.

"Have you ever thought about it?" he asked again. "I mean really thought about it? Have you ever thought it all the way through, back to the source of the problem, back to where it all began?

"Well," said Clive, looking slyly at Will Dysley with a quarter-century of vengeance in his eyes. His face broke into a determined smile. "I have. And this is what I've come up with."

Randell Clive then proceeded with a tremendously interesting dissertation, one that brought shock to the people who sat in the courtroom audience, including the members of Dysley's infamous *Legal Entourage,* who had never faced an opposing argument anything like the one they had just heard. It brought uncertainty to Elizabeth, the mother of Mary, as to whether or not this trial was entirely the right thing to do as Mr. Clive had insisted when she first met him, and it brought outrage to about half of the growing hordes of protesters watching the courtroom drama outside the courthouse on their miniature TV sets. The other half felt rather justified in what they heard.

The counsel's argument also brought extreme delight to the media managers, who immediately saw incredible opportunities for circulation-catching headlines and increased Nielsen ratings.

The only person who didn't seem to show any adverse reaction was opposing counselor Will Dysley. While the postargument ruckus erupted around him in the courtroom, he calmly, unperturbedly reached into his breast pocket and packed a fresh bowl of tobacco in his pipe. A thin, crafty smile spread across his aged face.

What they had all heard from the counsel for the plaintiff, what had caused all the shock and uncertainty, the outrage and delight, the immense variety of individual reaction, was precisely this:

"School, like this courtroom, is a place of fact. A place, like this courtroom, where everything we hear is weighed against the parameters of truth. Our children's textbooks are filled with what we, and our nation's greatest minds, consider the most accurate representation of the facts—proven facts about mathematics, geography, and the evidenced truths of history.

"For example, it is no longer appropriate to teach our children that the world is flat; that myth has been proven to be false. But at one time the idea of a flat world, which we consider to be so ludicrous, was taught to the children of the day in their schools. Now, however, we know the truth. We've sailed around the world, our aircraft have flown around the world, and our spaceships have seen the entire world from afar such that it appears like a small blue marble. We now know that the world is round.

"The myth of a flat world has dissolved away into a reality that we all now accept as the truth.

"Why, you may ask, is this relevant to the case of a little girl caught red-handed in the act of praying at the flagpole of her school?

"Because at the heart of Mary's prayer lies a myth like the one I've just mentioned—a myth that has never been subjected to an examination of truth and authenticity, never had itself dusted with the archaeologist's brush for fingerprints of proof.

"Never have men built great vessels and sailed over the horizon of this myth, hopeful that they would not fall off the edge of the Earth. As it was before the great adventurers set sail on their brave journeys, no one knows the reality behind the myth that is at the origin of Mary's innocent act. No one knows what truth awaits us.

"This is our great vessel, my friends—this court of law—to explore the reality that waits for us behind the myth that is, ultimately, the simple story of a missing body. A great mystery that has remained unsolved for nearly 2,000 years.

"In this trial, you and I will set sail on a great voyage of discovery. We will seek the evidence, we will seek the facts, we will seek the truth.

"And once we have the evidence for the reality behind the myth, the myth becomes no longer a myth, but a fact, a historical fact. Then, with the facts in hand, the appropriate changes can be made in history books around the world, changes that would make little Mary's act by the flagpole a crime no more.

"The myth of which I speak is a myth at the heart of the history of mankind, which is why the protesters have gathered outside these walls and across the continents.

It is a myth steeped in the folklore, fables, and prophecies of every civilization that ever graced the face of this Earth. It is a story that has brought generation after generation of people to its knees.

"And we, just like the adventurers of old, must cross this myth's horizon if we are to survive our future.

"The myth of which I speak is the resurrection of Jesus Christ, and it is up to us, through this trial, to uncover the reality and the truth that awaits us, to discover whether or not Mary's prayer at the flagpole was spoken in vain.

"In this trial I will attempt to prove the historical validity of the resurrection of Christ, so that we may abandon the mythology behind Christ's life, death, and resurrection, and accept it as part of the factual history of the world.

"After this trial, I suspect, none of us will ever be the same."

5

Warnings of a Fool

AN INCREDIBLY FIERCE north wind off frozen Lake Michigan battered the hearty morning business crowd as they attempted to walk between the stories-high wind tunnels of the city. February was always the worst month for the cold wind the city was famous for. This year's blasts, however, were the worst people could remember.

This winter, the wind seemed possessed.

The frozen lake seemed to not only further cool the already-cold air streaming down from the wilds of Canada, but also to zip it along, quickening its unhindered assault of the midwestern flatlands. Only the impenetrable steel and concrete of the Chicago city-state could stand in its path, causing violent eddies and furious swirls that shot down the streets between the buildings, disrupting the progress of any in their trajectory.

The winds had been so consistent this year that if you were to observe the street from a safe shelter, you would have trouble believing there was any wind at all. The streets themselves appeared clean. The debris and garbage from the gutters, which normally filled the air with each whip of the wind, was nowhere to be seen. It had been, instead, driven hard into places from which it could not be moved, wedged, or beaten by the force of a prior gust. All flags and other objects subject to the violent currents had either been removed or battened down securely so that they could not be tempted to flitter away. Even the clouds, it seemed, had trouble holding their position in the tempest from the north. The skies were deceptively clear as far as the eye could see.

One structure standing on a street corner, comprised not of concrete and steel but of flesh and blood, seemed to operate with the wind. It acted as a sounding board deepening the wind's incessant poundings, its wool-coated back absorbing the wrath of the raw blasts, only to release them as a more powerful and influential force from its front side.

The wind passing through this particular structure on the street corner caused the newspapers and magazines on the stand behind it to flitter wildly despite the attendant's efforts to keep them secure.

"Mr. Dysley," said the newsstand attendant through a narrow slit in the hood of his parka, "good morning, sir."

The attendant wore thick-lensed glasses surrounded by thick plastic brown frames. There were smears along the edges of the lenses that made them look as if he wiped them with his fingers to clean them. He also had a frozen driblet of spit attached to the fur-lined rim of his hood.

"Here's yous paper, sir," said the slow-witted attendant. "Sorry it's so winkled an all, but da wind, yous know." He blew into his hands, which were chafed and red from the wind.

"Yes," said Will Dysley distantly as he snatched the paper from the attendant with a leather-gloved hand.

"They say it might get ta ten below taday, wit da wind chill dat is," said the subnormal. Steam from his breath rose up to fog his glasses, momentarily obscuring his bulbous, distorted, owl-like eyes. A dirty, ink-stained finger quickly wiped away the condensation.

"Yes," said Will Dysley even more distantly as he opened the newspaper and quickly scanned the headline.

"Last time it were dis cold were back in '79. Whoa boy, dat were a cold one!" the attendant muddled about his stand, organizing the stacks of papers.

"I numember '79, don't yous, Mr. Dysley? Yous was standin' there, and I was standin' over here!" He burst into a moronic-sounding laugh. "Same as now!"

"Yes," said Will, still looking down at the front page of the newspaper only now with a portentous smile on his face. It had shown him, obviously, what he wanted to see.

It would be unfair to say that Dysley was ignoring the attendant simply because he was so intent on seeing what the media had written about the trial, because he had totally ignored this simpleminded man every business-day morning for the past fifteen years. Every morning the dim-witted attendant handed him a newspaper on his way to the office and made some awestruck comment about his professional achievements, and every morning Dysley, without exception, ignored him.

Dysley even neglected to make eye contact with the man he considered to be a blathering idiot. As it turned out, however, this was not a neglect left only for idiots.

A long time ago, Will Dysley had determined that eye contact, like fossil fuel, was a resource, and therefore, was not to be wasted. In fact, the personnel at his law firm had learned to respectfully ignore their employer, to thoughtfully forget about any idle morning salutations or coffeepot conversations with the monarchical boss.

Dysley's cold, calculated stares were reserved for those unfortunate enough to do combat with him in the courtroom, not for those he had no need to intimidate.

Even in the whipping wind, there was no mistaking the scent of body odor that now wafted past Will Dysley's nose. He looked upwind to see the source of the odor which hovered over his left shoulder.

"Dat's yous trial, huh, Mr. Dysley?" said the odor.

For the first time in fifteen years, Will looked at the newsstand attendant from his rubber galoshes to the sooty fur lining of his hood, all the while trying to ascertain meaning from the words, or rather, syllables that he had just heard. He realized in that brief moment that here, obviously, was a salesman who exercised flagrant disregard for the pronunciation of the words in the language in which he made his living. Will Dysley judged that he knew everything he needed to know about the newspaper attendant.

Dysley folded the newspaper, tucked it under his arm, and pushed past the irksome attendant. He stopped on the curb and looked up at the gothic spires of the *Tribune* building, the same building he saw through the windows of his penthouse office. Some people bumped by him struggling against the wind, trying to cross the street. He thought about how long that great building had stood as an integral part of the historic Chicago skyline. He stood in awe of the unique structure shaped with character and history rising like a massive redwood in a forest of lowly pines. He thought about how much he wanted to change the world, how he wanted an honored place alongside the men who comprised the skyline of history—how he wanted, like most men, for his name never to be forgotten.

With his gloved hand he gently tapped the newspaper folded under his arm and stepped down from the safety of the curb onto the icy street.

"Ahhh...Mr. Dysley!" cried the voice of a fool after his longtime customer, "Watch'yer step, sir! Be careful, sir! Watch'yer step!"

6

Scholars and Doubts

TWENTY-FIVE YEARS was a long time.

A long time since the union of two ambitious, young law school graduates had catalyzed the formation of a law partnership hell-bent on changing the world. By their tenth-year anniversary, the partners had accumulated enough wealth and clientele to move their offices to prestigious North Michigan Avenue and to commission a corporate sign.

The sign hung just above street level, facing North Michigan Avenue. It was comprised of nearly six tons of granite, uniquely chiseled and chased into cavernous folds, beautifully capturing the essence of the partners' inception pact. There it stood, an anaglyphic reminder to all who passed by, that the world had indeed changed as a result of the union of Will Dysley and Tom Weber, even if it was only some of the world's raw materials.

Will Dysley passed directly underneath the sign and pushed through the revolving doors of his Empire. He took the elevator to the top floor, where he was cordially ignored, just as he liked it, by the members of his staff that happened to be there as the elevator opened.

The employees could always tell who was new in the firm because the newcomers were typically the only ones who actually greeted "The Man" in the morning. They soon learned, and usually the hard way, about the firm's unwritten law.

"Good morning, Mr. Dysley!" yelled Bob Lapper over the heads of half the people on the floor. The employees snickered and quickly disappeared into their cubbyholes. The newest associate in the firm apparently had not been given any coaching by the other employees. "Quite a shocker in court yesterday, eh, Mr. Dysley? I don't think I would've been ready for that one!"

"Gladys!" shouted Will right through Bob Lapper. "Are *they* here yet?"

Lapper strode up next to Will, his corduroy pants meshing together and sounding like a playing card in the spokes of a bicycle wheel as he walked.

"Just the same, I'm glad it's you in there instead of me," said Lapper with the same childish grin he sported on that first day in Will's office. He tried to straighten the immensely too-large knot in his tremendously outdated tie. "Has Clive thrown a curve into this First Amendment stuff, or what?" he said, slapping Will on the back.

"Gladys!" said Will, glaring angrily at the grinning price he had to pay to put Magellan versus Longview

Elementary under his firm's jurisdiction. He had received no response from his office manager, who proficiently continued about her work. He shot another agitated look in her direction as he and Lapper strode by the main reception desk.

"Sir?" asked Gladys innocently. Will Dysley's office manager stopped what she was doing and looked up at her employer. When their eyes met, the middle-aged woman appeared to suddenly remember who the *they* were that her boss was asking about.

"Oh, them," she said with borderline feigned spontaneity. "Why yes, they're here, sir. They are waiting for you in the East Conference Room."

Will was unsure if Gladys, who was the sharpest secretary he had ever had, could actually not know immediately who the *they* were he was asking about, or if she just knew how to subtly get to him without showing blatant disrespect. If he could have done without her, which he couldn't, he thought he would have.

"Good," said Dysley as he walked briskly past the reception area. He tried to meet Gladys's eyes, but she had already returned to her work, her nose buried in a thick document. He thought he saw the corner of a smile as he stopped to look back at her while removing his long wool coat.

"Will you need any briefing on client history, Mr. Dysley?" offered Bob Lapper with uncharacteristic confidence.

Will looked startlingly at him as if to say, *You're still here?* And for the first time in Lapper's brief tenure with the firm, Dysley's eyes met square on with his.

Trapped for the moment by Dysley's acrimonious glower, Lapper could think to do nothing but study the man in front of him. He saw that he wore a finely tailored dark suit with a different, but equally conservative and not altogether boring tie. He also noticed that Dysley was not completely gray-haired, as he had originally seen him to be that evening in his office. Much of his head, he observed, was completely lacking of hair, but that didn't seem to matter in the least. He was the type of bald man who people didn't notice was bald unless it was pointed out for them directly, and whose baldness refused to detract from his distinguished looks or his overall presence—a presence which began to affect the newest member of the firm in discomforting waves of increasing frequency and modulation.

As displeased as he was with this morning's second intrusion, Will Dysley couldn't help himself. Every time he looked at Bob Lapper, he thought about the beautiful case that had dropped into his lap, a case he needed to put into his firm's venue at whatever the cost. Unfortunately, the cost was high; a highly sought after associate position in the firm, filled with amazing perks. Bob Lapper's face, he thought, was a face that he would have to look at for quite some time to come. The associate position entitled him to at minimum, a ten-year tenure with the firm, as well as a ticket to every board meeting, every executive meeting, every shareholder's meeting, and every single one of the political functions sponsored by the firm.

The thought of Bob Lapper in any social setting, let alone one of his parties, made Will's stomach boil. So, without saying a word, he simply plastered a smile on his face and tapped Lapper on the shoulder and handed him his overcoat. He then walked off toward the East Conference Room.

Bob Lapper stood dumbfounded, staring down at the heavy coat draped over his arm. He looked at Gladys, who had watched the whole degrading episode, but pretended not to have seen a thing. She licked her finger and turned the page of the document before her. The head honcho, she thought jokingly to herself, had wasted no time in showing the new man his function in the day-to-day workings of the firm.

Tom Weber sauntered out of his office, his face hidden behind the morning edition. He had worked up a couple of nice rings of sweat under his armpits for this early in the morning. His pudgy cheeks always looked pink, but this morning they took on a slightly brighter hue which tended more toward red. He took short little steps down the hallway, blind as he was while absorbing the articles written about the trial.

"Got to hand it to you, Will," he said without putting the newspaper down, "I don't think the media knows if there's weather today, nor do they seem to care."

To a casual onlooker, Tom's perceptive abilities would have seemed unnatural just then. Somehow he knew it was Will who was striding down the hall toward him, and he knew precisely when to speak his words of greeting. But Will, who had grown used to his partner, knew that it wasn't so much keen perception that had guided Tom Weber as it was extreme worry. He knew his partner had been waiting to hear his telltale stride clicking down the marble-floored hallway; he knew that his partner would have something to say about the incredibly controversial press their case was getting.

One good turn deserves another, he thought, and he threw up his copy of the *Tribune* so that the front-page headline faced his partner.

It read: "DYSLEY, CLIVE PUT JESUS ON TRIAL!"

"You sure know how to pick 'em," said Tom softly as he peered over his bifocals at the large type striped across the page. Further down he read some of the subheads: "History and Christ Come Together in Trial," "Two-Thousand-Year-Old Hoax or Miracle?" "The Burden of Proof, a Heavy Cross to Bear," and "Dysley Firm to Oppose Christ."

"We're right where we should be, Tom," said Will triumphantly. "Right there in the thick of things" he said as he jabbed the newspaper with his index finger, denting it.

"You're ecstatic about this?" said Tom disbelievingly.

"Of course I am. This case is good for the firm and good for the people of the world. It was all inevitable, Tom; surely you can see that? Just be glad we have a hand in it all. I'd hate to be on the sidelines watching history unfurl before our eyes. Now, come on, man, *they* are already here and waiting for us."

Will started down the hall. Tom followed with a look of dread on his face.

"I really want to talk with you after the meeting, Will," he said. "You've been acting rather strangely about this case, and I don't think it's all the attention you're getting. Heaven knows you should be used to that by now!"

"We'll talk, we'll talk." Will's voice trailed off as he disappeared around the corner. He respectfully waited for his partner to arrive at the door to the East Conference Room so that they could enter together. When Tom finally got there shaking his head, he pushed open the door.

What greeted them was the suffocating smell of musty old books. The smell was overpowering and actually caused them to reel backwards on their heels. When they recovered, they looked upon a group of bearded men dressed in drab, ill-fitting suits, sitting at the conference table.

The creak of the door must have alerted the men, who almost in unison looked up from the books they were reading. Every one of them wore glasses, and when they turned their faces upward their glasses caught the fluorescent lighting from above, making their eyes look like large white orbs.

Piled next to these odd creatures was volume after volume of what appeared to be ancient texts and manuscripts. Scattered around the table were loose sheets of yellowed, delicate parchment, and next to them were rolls of old cracked leather filled with writing.

Will entered the room without saying a word to the seated men; he was awestruck by the apparent age of the leather and the paper. Never had he seen anything that percolated antiquity like these books. He went to the table and gently lifted one of the old sheets of leather. Along its edge he could see where holes had been punched in the leather, holes now stretched and ripped through. He wondered where the covers that had once bound the individual sheets had gone, how the leather pages must have one day been attached to large covers, and binded with huge metal rings. It was as if the ancient knowledge held by the decaying rolls had grown with the speculation and conjecture of the many readers over the years, growing beyond that which could be bound by a cover.

Will noticed that some pages were not complete. They were torn or fragmented as if they had become weary of burning candles and searching eyes and had chosen rather to give in to the properties of time, to shirk their duty to pass along wisdom, and to carry away forever the mysteries they held. Will felt a strange impulse to absorb the mysteries inscribed into the parchment before they vanished into disintegrating flakes of leather and ink—mysteries he could not allow to pass from his grasp; myths and mysteries he was determined to piece together.

"Gentlemen," said Will, looking up from his inspired search. "I am Will Dysley, and this is my partner Tom Weber."

Tom smiled and nodded cordially to the dusty-looking old men seated around the table. Behind his smile, a thought flashed across his mind. Which of the receptacles of knowledge, he wondered, were the origin of the musty odor that filled the room; the paper and leather ones, or the human ones?

"Thank you for coming," said Tom pleasantly, widening his smile, ashamed of what had just crossed his mind. "I'm sorry we couldn't explain the reason we wanted you here today, but we had to wait until after the opening argument yesterday. We appreciate your..." he looked timidly over at his partner, "...blind faith."

"Yes," said Dysley, anxious to get things rolling. "You gentlemen are the world's foremost biblical archaeologists, paleographers, Qumranologists, textual critics, and cryptologists. Most of you have devoted your lives to the study of people and events in and around ancient Palestine."

Will began to circle the table, the scholars' eyes followed him, the white orbish reflections in their glasses changing shapes as they turned their heads.

"You are all no doubt well-read individuals," he continued, tapping one of the tall stacks of manuscripts, "so I do not feel like you need me to explain what this is all about.

"You have all been asked to come here for one reason. It is not important that you agree with what we are asking you to do, but only that you do it. To some of you it may appear as if we are embarking on a sacrilegious journey, having been forced by the argumental posturing of counsel for the plaintiff to oppose Jesus Christ.

"That is not my desire," said Will.

Tom looked at Will in shock. "However," Will continued, "we are faced with a moral dilemma. Due process must be done if we are to have any hope of preserving the Constitution as it relates to public displays of religion. It is too late to turn back. If you feel that you are incapable of following through with the research we request, then I urge you to pick up your things and leave through that door."

The roomful of introverted polymaths remained silent, staring intently at the master orator. Except for one.

The man who stood up at the table just then was easily the most contemporarily dressed of the entire group, although he had to be in his seventies. He dressed as if he still cared about the world outside of his mind, a rare characteristic among history's great scholars and scientists, and definitely lacking in any of his peers gathered around the conference table.

He pushed himself to his feet with a polished mahogany walking stick that curlicued at the end where he gripped it. In his free hand he held an olive-colored fedora with a small black-and-yellow feather snugged into the strap around the brim.

"If you'll excuse me, Mr. Dysley, Mr. Weber," said the well-dressed man nodding respectfully as he started for the door. Tom Weber unraveled the handkerchief he had balled up in his fist and nervously wiped the sweat from his forehead.

Will continued unperturbed by the distraction, directing his comments at the old scholar heading for the exit.

"But I warn you," he said earnestly, "the mass-media exposure of this sacred myth of the resurrection has already disrupted your quiet studies. The trial has shed the light of mainstream society onto your back room beliefs and hypotheses. They will no longer stand in the face of the questions of the people. This is no longer a subject reserved for scholars and scientists.

"The cat, you might say, is out of the bag."

The old man, who was just about ready to turn the door handle, stopped in his tracks. A thought had occurred to him, a thought rooted in perception and an understanding of human need. He turned around humbly and returned to his seat at the table.

Will waited for the old scholar to sit back down.

A sense of relief seemed to envelope Tom. He took in a deep breath and jammed his crumpled handkerchief into his pocket.

"Those of you who choose to stay will become part of a newfound religious agenda," Dysley continued. "You will have a hand in shaping the new understanding that the world public will soon demand." He had completely circled the table and now stood next to his partner.

"What we ask of you is very simple," he said. He looked at Tom and put his hand on his shoulder. "We would like you to think back through all of your travels and locate your personal notes on the ancient manuscripts you have read over the years. We would like you to recall what many of you probably wish you had never experienced. Namely, your battles with skepticism, agnostic thoughts, and doubt concerning the story of the resurrection of Jesus Christ.

"We would like you to try to remember the source of your anxiety, whether it was an inconsistency that you read in the Bible, chatter from a back alley in Jerusalem, or whisperings from your own subconscious." Will Dysley stretched his chin tight.

"I want the *loose nail in the cross at Calvary!*" he said almost haughtily.

The old scholar who had almost left a minute ago studied Will closely. He toyed with his cane under the table and confirmed to himself that he had done the right thing by staying and remaining a part of the trial.

Tom Weber had never seen his partner so entirely engrossed with a case, neither had he seen him so perfectly eloquent in his words.

Tom waited long enough to make sure Will was finished speaking to the gathered scholars. "Any questions?" he asked politely.

He paused a minute, but got no response. Some of the scholars jotted down notes on the legal pads laid for them at each place at the table, others even looked somewhat excited about the prospect of setting out to solve the greatest mystery in all of history. Tom clapped his hands once and rubbed them together.

"Well," he said, "if you will all come with me, I'll show you to the research department. You can see Gladys up front for your hotel accommodations. We've got until next Monday to come up with an argument for our defense."

Tom caught Will's eyes motioning him to step outside. He held the door open for his partner. When the door had clicked shut behind them, Will looked at Tom with apprehension.

"Well," he inquired, "which one's it going to be?"

"Renshaw," said Tom convincingly, "we almost lost him in there."

"You mean he was..."

"Yes, he was the one who got up to leave the room. Professor Rubin Renshaw," said Tom, leafing through a vanilla envelope full of papers. "Twenty years as head archaeologist of biblical archives at the Smithsonian

Institute, authenticity supervisor of the Dead Sea Scrolls project in Israel, more degrees than even you, Will. He's credible all right, very credible. He's also a human being, and not so much of a hermit like the others. All we need is an expert witness who looks like one of the homeless. Renshaw's definitely our man."

Will took out his pipe and searched his breast pocket for a book of matches.

"Get him prepped for the stand, Tom," he said confidently, clenching the stem of his pipe between his teeth. "Clive is going to wish he gave up his vendetta twenty-five years ago. He should know I never forget a challenge."

Somehow Dysley's words did not ring of complete truth to his longtime partner. Tom almost felt like asking him if he was holding something back, if there was something Will wasn't telling him.

Just then the door to the conference room swung open, and that same musty scent wafted past Tom's nose. Pushing the smell before them was the group of scholars for hire, lugging their stacks of ancient manuscripts with them. They looked to Tom for direction to the room where they could do what they loved most: research.

Professor Rubin Renshaw lagged back from the others. He slowly made his way by the two partners, using his mahogany cane for support. He had a consenting smile on his face when Tom asked him to step into his office for a chat.

7

Presents and Eggs

WILL DYSLEY simply could not believe this was happening to him.

There was far from anything good-natured in the way he had driven his Lincoln Continental from his downtown office to the Angel of Mercy Hospital on the outskirts of the city. He needed this time to prepare for the most important trial of his life, not this. Not at all. And didn't she know that?

Will Dysley was a man with little tolerance for interruption or distraction in his life. His focus had always been on the law and the cases he had going at the time. And now, with the upcoming megatrial, his time was gold—pure gold.

The woman whose hospital bed he now sat upon knew that fact very well.

Will had tried to give her the benefit of the doubt. Samantha Hollimon was not the type of woman who would do something rash or absurd to make sure she was part of his daily routine. An ongoing relationship for the past seven years had taught him that much about her. Her last-minute request made with a desperate phone call to his office that afternoon was definitely for real. If she would have had a choice, Will felt sure she would have taken it. Things as they were, however, with the case begging for his undivided attention, Will could not even pretend he was accepting of her request, as ludicrous as it was. The mere thought of it made him want to crawl through his skin and leave his limp exoskeleton on the bed. The only reason he didn't was because of the place where he was, or more precisely, the place where she was. The place where Samantha Hollimon had spent the past week.

The Angel of Mercy Hospital, whose physicians still did not have a clue as to what was wrong with her.

"I'm sorry, honey," said Samantha in a regretful whisper, "but I have no other option."

Samantha Hollimon was forty-two and a rather attractive woman even after having spent the past seven days in a hospital bed. She had other endearing qualities about her as well, marked by a light, pleasant demeanor and an overall aversion to moodiness in any form. Thus it was exceedingly difficult for her to be laid up the way she was with an unknown intruder attacking her central nervous system and demanding at least moderate, contemplative mood swings. She was not an educated woman in the academic sense, but she was filled with the intuitive knowledge of life, which was perhaps the main reason Will Dysley had been and still was attracted to her.

As Will studied her appearance he noticed that despite her extended illness, Sam's skin had retained the almost ageless smoothness that he had always known it to have. It was only her auburn hair that showed any signs of the trauma which faced her, taking on that hospital look; it was flat and wet from worry and plastered around her forehead, and it had that bland, plaintive odor, a bit like a wet puppy. She wore her own nightshirt as people tend to do when they are in a hospital for more than a couple nights. The nightshirt was mainly white, with washed-out pastel floral patterns. She pulled it tight over her knees and gave Will her best empathic smile.

Will turned away, not letting her catch his eye.

He looked rather at the source of his frustration, the reason this had all become necessary in the first place.

There it was, already starting to annoy him with the constant flipping of the television channels. It lay stomach-down on the floor, legs bent at the knee, feet in the air, its oversized hightop tennis shoes rhythmically clapping together. The untied laces slapped lazily against the hard shoe leather, carelessly mocking the seriousness of Will's predicament. Each channel was allowed a short burst of sound before it was clicked to the next. The shrill voice of an actress in a daytime soap screaming at her boyfriend, the drum-rolling thunder of an ad for an exciting new car, the grating, penetrating voice of a salesman rattling off the latest discount prices for home appliances.

The creator of the annoyance could see that her man was near the breaking point. "Tyler!" she said firmly. "Honey, that's enough with the TV."

Ten-year-old Tyler Hollimon looked over his shoulder at his mother. He seemed to be trying to gauge the exact intent of her words. He then turned back around on his elbows, flipped the channel one more time from a daytime soap to a cartoon, and didn't change it again. He had guessed correctly that it was the channel-changing and not the watching of the TV for which he was being reprimanded. He lay there on the floor quietly watching the cartoon.

From behind, Samantha and Will saw him push back his thick strawberry-blond hair, which was bowl-cut and long in the back. They watched it fall neatly into place.

"I know it couldn't be a worse time," whispered Samantha, taking hold of Will's hand. "My mom is out of town, Marge is out of town, and I just don't trust anyone else. It's just until my mom gets back." She looked lovingly at her son in his new green sweater she had given him for Christmas. "He shouldn't be too much trouble..." Samantha's voice trailed off. She looked ready to burst into tears.

"Sam?" said Will, turning sharply toward her.

Tyler snapped round to see what was wrong.

"I'm OK," she said and took a deep breath. "I just get scared sometimes when I can't feel anything in my legs..." Tears that had been welling in her eyelids spilled over the edge. "Wouldn't you?" she snapped defensively.

"Easy now, Sam," said Will with a steady tone. "They're still totally numb?" He touched her leg below the knee and massaged it gently.

"Yes," she said, holding back a sniffle.

"How far up?"

"Sometimes just to my knees, sometimes all the way to my waist. Makes it hard to..." she motioned to the bathroom door, then reached for a tissue on the table.

"The MRI showed nothing?" asked Will, handing her his handkerchief.

"No," Sam shook her head trying to regain control of her nerves. "But they haven't done the one for my head yet, only the one for my spine." She looked at Tyler, who still stared at her beset with worry. "Don't ask me why they didn't do them both at once, that remains a *mystery of modern medicine.*" She gave out a lifeless chuckle.

"Something's blocking communication from the ol' noggin to my legs. They'll find it," she said, her reassurance directed at Tyler. "I know they'll find it." Sam tried to smile at her young son. Her bright smile had lost a lot of its light.

Tyler turned back around to the television.

"How long, Sam?" Will asked with concern.

"They don't know. Dr. Milan thinks..."

"I'm sorry, Sam," Will interrupted, "but I meant how long will Tyler be staying with me?"

"Oh...well." Samantha Hollimon tried to remain poised as her anger began to swell. "Since it would not be good for me to get angry right now, especially in my condition, I won't. I'll pretend that you didn't say that just then, and that you were really asking about how long I'll be cooped up in this darn bed!" She looked at Will, eyes burning with frustration and the potential of a mental breakdown.

....

"Dr. Milan," she said, demanding Will's direct and full attention, "thinks about one more week of testing should reveal whatever it is, then I can go home. As for the question *you did not* ask, but I'm sure you would be interested in, my mother will be home next Wednesday. And that, my irresponsible *manfriend,* will mark the end of your duty to me and my child." Sam quickly flipped over on her side, putting her back to her visitor.

Will let out a muffled, embarrassed laugh.

"It must be the trial," he said, "it's occupying my thoughts." He stood up and jammed his hands into his pockets. "This is the big one," Will peeked between the blinds to the hospital parking lot below. "The one I've been waiting for, honey."

Sam smiled girlishly while still facing the wall. Without turning around, she thrust her left hand in the air and wiggled her ring finger.

"Does that mean after this big one, it's time for *this* big one?" she asked.

He gave her a tight-lipped smile but did not answer.

Will knew that he and Sam were long overdue for the solidification of their union, and at ages fifty-eight and forty-two, he realized that they didn't have all the time in the world. They had both been through unsuccessful marriages in the past, which had somehow sufficed for an excuse to wait for the first five years of their relationship. But that excuse just sort of lost validity in the sixth year, leaving a kind of reasonless void. A void they had been floating mindlessly in for over two years now, leaving them unable to define or describe the type of relationship they had to any of their friends. Awkward terms

....

like "manfriend" and "lady o' mine" started surfacing and had slowly become part of their vocabularies. Sam's subtle and less-than-subtle reminders were all done good-naturedly, but Will knew that underneath, she was starting to get a little worried.

Sam had met Will on a fluke invite to one of the firm's political functions, when Tyler was three years old. It hadn't taken her long to ascertain the role she would play in the life of the renowned attorney Will Dysley, but she had to admit her motivations were not much different than his in the initial years of their relationship. A slender body, a welcoming smile, and practiced social graces were his, a distinguished man of means and influence were hers, and just as the passing of the decades began to thin the ranks on her desirability and for each, companionship without the imposition of familial duties. But that was sure to change and it had—for her, at least.

But as for Will, she could not be sure. Here was a man who was by now certainly set in his ways, a man who had grown accustomed to a life of solitude and privacy of thought. She could no more guess where his head was on a given subject than his highly trained lawyerly opponents could guess his conclusion to a line of questioning on a witness. His head was currently engrossed in a trial; that much she knew. She also sensed that this trial held a particular fascination for him—it apparently held an answer he had been seeking, although she wasn't sure to what question.

"Hey, Mom," said Tyler, excitedly popping to his feet and leaping onto his mother's bed, "is Mr. D gonna take me to church on Sunday?"

Sam pretended to bite her nails in fear.

"Oh, boy," she said nervously, "your mother forgot all about that one, kid." She looked qualmishly at Will. "Maybe if we ask Mr. D real nice, and tell him how you're in confirmation class at church and you're not allowed to miss a Sunday morning service, he will be kind enough to take you."

"Samantha, please!" Will demanded. "That's the day before my opening argument. The eyes of the world will be upon me!" He shook his head in contemplation of yet another forced interruption to his work. "Enough is enough!" he shouted.

Sam thought hard for a moment. She began to stroke Tyler's hair. She *looked* at her son but *talked* to the man she loved.

"Maybe Mr. D will realize that his trial involves the same Person you're learning about in class, and maybe he will realize that he might learn something in church on Sunday, something that might actually help him in his case."

"It's out of the question!" Will growled. "Case closed!" he said with a curt smile. He motioned with his thumb toward the door. "I'll be in the hall waiting for Tyler. I'll call you later this evening, Samantha, to see how you're doing." He tried to sound caring, but it came out like more trying was going on than actual caring.

Tyler put his head down and looked dejectedly at his mother.

"Get your stuff together, Tyler," she said tenderly. "Mr. D has a lot of work to do. He's a very important man." Tyler continued to look sadly at the floor.

"Hey, Mom," said Tyler weakly as he scuffed his high-top along the floor so it made a melancholy screech. He looked at the doorway to make sure Will could not see him, then burst into an ear-to-ear grin, showing two overly large upper-front teeth. He leaned in close to his mother. "He's one of them guys who prays fer presents and eggs, isn't he?"

"Tyler?" warned Sam, who then smiled wide at her son. She knew he was too clever for his age. "Don't start with your jokes. Mr. D is not in the mood for jokes just now."

Samantha Hollimon knew that her son was bright despite having what she considered to be half-bad genetics, which meant of course, from his father's side. The same father that had left them when Tyler was an infant. *Maybe,* she thought, *his father's absence had forced the boy to mature more quickly and that maturity had brought about his keen sense of humor?* However plausible that theory was, she quickly dismissed it, not wanting to give the deserting dad credit for anything, even if it was credit given due to his absence.

She couldn't say, however, that Will had stepped right in to take over the fatherly role. It wasn't as if he and Tyler didn't get along; it was more like they never *were* along, or rather, if one of them was, the other wasn't.

Tyler didn't go with them on their weekend getaways to the North Woods of Wisconsin or the Upper Peninsula of Michigan, and Will didn't go along when Samantha had family duties to attend to, which included family Christmas parties or any holiday get-togethers. As a result, the man and the boy had never really gotten to know each other in the seven years that Will had been seeing her.

However, circumstances as they were, this seemed destined to change. Sam only hoped that Will could cope with a ten-year-old with the wit of Chevy Chase.

"He is, huh?" asked Tyler with a smart-mouthed grin on his face.

"Stop," Tyler's mother barely got out the word before she exploded into a short burst of laughter. "What the heck does that mean anyway?" she asked, trying to hold back another fit.

"Aw, come on! You remember, Mom? He's a twice-a-yearer at church! Presents and eggs!" Tyler stood back from the bed and spread open his arms. "He only prays for Christmas presents and Easter eggs!" he emphasized. "Just like Jimmie and his family!"

Sam threw back her head in laughter. "That's not nice!" she said giggling. "Where did you get that from?"

Tyler slapped the bed and joined in with a high-pitched laugh.

Will peeked through the doorway to see what all the ruckus was about.

Tyler, bent over with his arms on the bed, looked under his elbow at Will in the doorway and quickly changed his laughter to sobbing. He stood up and faced Will with his eyes wet from laughter. He flipped his smile over to a frown and rubbed the tears away with the back of his hand.

"I'm ready," he said sadly, peering up at Will with a painful twist on his face. "I'm ready to go, Mr. D," he managed in between manufactured sobs.

Will rolled his eyes upward and turned back toward the hall.

Sam and Tyler shared one more brief smile.

"Come here, you little actor," said Sam adoringly. "Don't you bother Mr. D too much now," she added, hugging him and trying for a serious voice.

"I won't, Mom," said Tyler obediently, scuffing his shoe against the floor again. "I won't make any promises, that is!" he laughed, grabbing his bag and running toward the doorway. "Pray fer them eggs!" he yelled as he disappeared through the doorway.

Samantha Hollimon winced and pulled the bedsheet over her head.

8

The Wind and the Tree

TYLER HOLLIMON thought for a moment that it was odd that he had never been to this mansion before, given the length of time his mother had been seeing its owner, or maybe it was just that he had been too young to remember being brought here. The thought crossed his mind but did not linger long, mainly because one key word within the preceding thought was much more enticing to a ten-year-old boy than any contemplation of hurt feelings. And that word was *mansion!*

Tyler smiled to himself. This place was huge, he thought. There was simply too much exploring to be done to spend time worrying about his mother's reasons for never having brought him here before.

Tyler had long ago lost the scent of pipe smoke he had been following through the house, the scent that he knew could care less whether he followed it or not. He had the general idea where Mr. D and his pipe had dropped his bags. It was a room at the top of the stairs, just to the left. He logged that in and was gone.

The backyard was where he began his exploration, a safe distance from the museum-like perfection of the furnishings of the interior of the house. Back there, where there was no danger of smudging the carpet or breaking a lamp. Back there, where he could burn off the steam that had been building inside of him throughout the day. He wasn't used to being in hospitals and cars all day, especially on a winter day like this.

The day had somewhat of an ominous appeal to it. It was the type of day during which little girls love to stay inside safe and warm, and imagine extravagant romances in the lives of their dolls, but which little boys find strangely attractive outside. The blue, mile-high skies and the cold winter sun cast a different light on the familiar landscapes of play. The winter had yielded little snow this year, but plenty of cold and wind, wind that had been driving ceaselessly for days, whipping and stirring the landscape, further drawing Tyler irresistibly to it. Tyler didn't care that all that remained was maybe an hour or so of fading light. He still needed to make his mark on this day; he felt compelled to make it, in some way, his.

His hightops squealed as he busted out of the back door of the large kitchen of Will Dysley's mansion, launching himself onto the hard frozen ground of the backyard.

"No way!" he yelled as he rolled over, crunching the stiff grass. He looked up from ground level at the rest of the yard stretching out in a sheet of matted gray-green grass. Scattered clumps of ice and snow, hardened and worn smooth by the wind, stood like sentinels at the four corners of the yard, perfectly marking the end zones of an imaginary playing field. He and his mother had been living in a modest apartment in the city with no yard to speak of since his father had left them. He and his buddies had to go all the way to what they called "the churchyard" to play football because it was just that— the yard to the side of the church. This yard, he was sure, had room enough for a five-on-five!

Tyler's excitement could hardly be contained. He shot off around the yard running imaginary patterns, avoiding imaginary tackles, and catching imaginary passes. The yard had tons and tons of fallen leaves everywhere, perfect for tumbling kids diving for end zones. His enthusiasm continued to build, until on a split-left pattern, he nearly ran smack-dab into the source of all those leaves.

Tyler was barely able to stop his forward progress. His nose stopped just short of getting flattened by massive sheets of frozen bark. From this vantage point, he looked straight up.

His mouth fell open.

Never had he seen such an awesome sight! This was easily the largest tree he had ever seen!

Tyler didn't know it, but he was staring up at an ancient winter oak tree, and probably one of the oldest survivors of the invasion of the suburbanites into the oak forests of Illinois. He leaned back away from the tree to try to see the top. He saw the winter-dead limbs of the tree twisting away from the main trunk. A sudden gust of the chilling north wind caused the scraggled, contorted limbs to sway and rattle against one another, as if they were struggling to free themselves from their invisible captor.

In an instant of imagination the bulbous black shapes above became a hundred horses, black horses, silhouetted against the waning light of the evening. The steeds had been frozen while trying to escape the merciless, invisible force that had struck so suddenly, preserving them in the throes of their contorted battle postures.

A frightening chill ran the length of Tyler's spine.

His mind flashed to his toy room at home, where he had miniature Roman warriors on horseback. He wondered where the horsemen on the wraith-like mounts in the great tree had gone. Had they been thrown by the crazed stallions? Had they escaped?

Tyler's thoughts were rewarded with another slash of wind, so fierce that he could almost hear the neighing and thrashing of the helpless horses trapped in their seasonal prison. A leaf long since dead was carried by the cold wind until it slapped onto Tyler's face and was stuck there momentarily. He had to reach up and pull it off his cheek.

Tyler's eyes grew wide. He looked at the leaf in horror.

Here was a horseman, he thought.

Then he was certain that a battle had taken place.

He saw the horsemen dressed in full battle colors struggling valiantly against the seasonal intruder. He saw them ripped from their loyal mounts and thrown down to the ground, broken and dead. Their carcasses littered the yard, decaying and disintegrating, the bright yellows, oranges, and reds of their battle cloaks becoming soiled and dull. Death was everywhere in the yard. Still their loyal mounts lived on deep within the core of their existence, but only on the terms of the intruder, their freedom governed by the grinding cogs and rasping wheels of some concealed, imperceptible timepiece.

"Tyler!" rang a voice from behind him. A voice carried by the wind.

Frightened, Tyler bolted for the voice which he did not recognize but was willing to accept over the scene that faced him at the tree.

"Tyler! Where are you, boy?"

Tyler recognized the voice and ran even faster to it. The voice did not elicit a feeling of comfort, but anything was better than the wind and the tree.

"Coming, Mr. D," Tyler managed between short, exaggerated breaths.

"What are you doing out here, boy?" said Will as Tyler leapt over the barren flower boxes lining the backyard patio. He stopped outside the kitchen door.

"Nothin', Mr. D," said Tyler, out of breath.

"Where were you, kid? I thought you were trying to get me in trouble with your mother already. You sure you're all right?"

"Yeah, Mr. D, just like they say in the deodorant commercials, 'No sweat'! What's fer dinner?" Tyler pushed past Will into the kitchen.

Will shook his head and closed the door behind him, but not before a serpentine blast of cold air slipped past him along the floor. "Looks like Martha left us something in the oven, Tyler. You can help yourself; I'm not hungry right now."

Tyler leaned against the counter, still shaken from his experience in the yard. He remained in constant motion, flipping his hair back and rubbing his hands together so that Will would not see him shake. "Sounds like a winner, Mr. D," he said as cheerily as he could muster.

"Good. I'm sure your mother told you that I have a lot of work to do. I'll be in my study," Will motioned with a nod to the room down the hallway at the other end of the house. "You can go up to your room and watch some TV after dinner."

Tyler nodded appreciatively and gave Will a weak smile. He looked around despairingly at the large white-tile kitchen, suddenly willing to sacrifice the exploration of this new world for the cramped comfort of his own apartment with its small kitchen, where he wished he stood side by side with his mother as she prepared his favorite meal.

Will walked out of the kitchen and down the long hallway to his study.

Tyler Hollimon realized just then that he missed his mother very much. He was frightened for her and for himself. He didn't know what he would do if his mother never got better. He tried not to think about how his life would change if his mother never came home from the hospital.

9

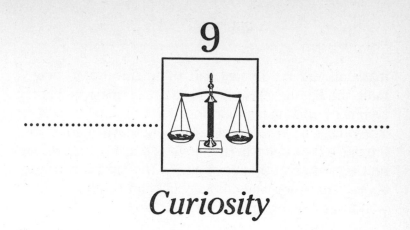

Curiosity

"HOW COME God's on money?"

Will stooped over the old wood-burning stove behind his desk in the study, arranging and poking a couple of fresh logs. He had paid a group of scholars very handsomely for the report that sat on his desk, the contents of which he now turned over in his mind. He was aware that the report had been compiled under considerable trepidation. It could not have been easy for these men, who had spent their lives in pursuit of biblical truths and justifications for their faith, to recall and record their innermost questions and doubts about the story of Christ's resurrection for the sake of the trial.

Like it or not, however, the scholarly men had done what Will had requested and, it appeared by the thickness of the report, compiled a substantial amount of material. Material Dysley had sifted through to determine the best angle at which to attack his opponent's argument on Monday morning.

Will had been so intent in his work that he had let the fire die to the point where there was only hot orange ash on the bottom of the stove cavity. His back was to the door of the study, and all his poking and shifting of the wood was making quite a bit of noise.

"How come God's on money?"

Will continued to poke at the new logs trying to get the fire going, all the while preoccupied with establishing a common cord or pattern from the complex, soul-searching dissertations of the hired scholars. It was late, probably past midnight, much too late for that to have been what he thought it was.

"How come God's on money?"

This time Will stopped his poking. In the silence, infant flames arose from the orange ash around the new logs in the fire, delightfully exploring the underbelly of their newfound fuel.

"Do you know, Mr. D?" said a tiny voice, and this time unmistakably. The voice seemed to echo the curiosity of the flames in the stove.

Like a small pebble's disturbance of a placid pool, Will lost the late-night tranquility of his thoughts. What he had thought it much too late for, and had dismissed as an impossibility, was indeed happening. He turned with a raised eyebrow to see what and who he knew to be the source of that impossibility.

There, in the doorway, stood Tyler Hollimon in his red cotton pajamas complete with booties—booties that padded along the smooth wood floor of the study and leapt into a soft leather reclining chair. Tyler's face flickered in the firelight, his wide-alert eyes were moist and glistening and telling Will that here was a child who should have been asleep four or more hours ago, but who was, obviously, very much awake.

"Tyler," said Will, straightening up and turning to face the late-night visitor, "you should not be up at this hour."

"Look, Mr. D," Tyler picked up a coin from the palm of his hand and displayed it between his fingers. "It says right here, under this guy's chin."

Will sat back down at his desk.

"It says, 'In God We Trust,'" said Tyler curiously. He reclined the chair to its full horizontal position while he studied the coin. Will picked up his pen and went back to his research trying to regain his line of thought, hoping desperately that the inquisitive nuisance would just go away.

"How can our money *trust God?*" said Tyler doubtfully, his face contorted in perplexity.

"Tyler," said Will in his best corrective tone.

"D'zat make money religious?" asked Tyler.

Will set down his pen and looked at the boy. Tyler bounced his legs as he lay back in the chair. The soft leather puffed with every impact. His red booties elongated away from his feet.

"I mean, if our money trusts God, then it must be religious. Right, Mr. D?"

How should this be handled? thought Will. He knew how to handle clients, jurists, judges, a law firm with 400 personnel, but he had limited experience with children. His marriage had ended without the most remote inclination of a bouncing baby coming down the pike.

Will decided to fall back on what he knew. He would try leading the witness.

"Why don't you ask your teacher in confirmation class?"

"Pastor."

"What did you call me?"

"Don't have a teacher, have a pastor."

The wood in the stove crackled.

"Ask your pastor, then," said Will calmly as he picked up his pen again. "Now boy, up to bed."

"The date, too," said Tyler, continuing to study the coin and ignoring Will's directive.

Inadmissible, thought Will, ignoring Tyler.

"The date means after Jesus' birthday," said Tyler pensively. "At least that's what pastor says. He says even people who don't believe in Jesus, when they write the date, are sayin' they do." Tyler let out a short laugh.

He would go for recrimination.

"Tyler," said Will firmly, "your mother is going to find out about this unless you get up to bed."

"In school, too," said Tyler, flipping the coin in the air. "God's everywhere."

"What?" Will was actually a little curious.

"In school, in the pledge of allegiance. You know, 'One nation under God, with liberty, and justice for...'"

"Tyler!" shouted Will authoritatively.

"...all."

Will thought he really didn't need this.

"Hey," said Tyler suddenly, "our money *trusts* God, and our nation's *under* God..."

Perhaps plea bargaining?

"Please, Tyler," Will begged.

"And in the 'aug-ur-a-tion,'" Tyler struggled with the word. "President's left hand goes on it." Tyler raised his right hand like he was being sworn into office.

"What?"

"The Bible."

"The Bible?"

"Yeah, when he moves into the White House, he puts his left hand on the Bible. Hey," it dawned on Tyler, "d'zat mean all presidents are religious?"

Settlement?

"OK, Tyler," said Will, pushing himself up from the desk. "I won't tell your mom that you stayed up so late if you'll go upstairs right now."

Tyler weighed the settlement. Mr. D, he thought, was on the run.

"Will you take me to church tomorrow?" he said coyly and hopped out of the chair.

"I've too much to do," said Will, nudging Tyler toward the doorway.

A possible continuance?

"Lots of people swear to God, too," Tyler began as if he could go on forever. "How come they do that, Mr. D? What do they mean by that? Pastor says we're not supposed to..."

Restitution.

"What time's church?"

"9:30."

Will walked Tyler upstairs to his room to make sure he got to bed sometime before dawn. "The reason I need to go tomorrow is because we get our Bibles tomorrow!" Tyler explained excitedly, jumping two steps at once. "All the kids in the confirmation class get them! Ain't that neat, Mr. D?"

"Yes, Tyler, that's neat," said Will solemnly. "We got ours when we were twelve, aren't you a little you...?" Will stopped himself.

Tyler looked up at him, astonished.

"Got what?" he said. "You got a Bible, too?"

It took a moment for the blurry memory to clarify.

"Once...yes," said Will, sort of surprised that he remembered that just then. And Will's mind began to peel away the thick, matted layers of vegetation accumulated from nearly fifty years of memory lopped on top of memory. Like a rain forest canopy which blocks the light, the memory of Will's childhood confirmation class and his childhood Bible had remained safely hidden in the dark reaches of his mind.

Until this moment with the boy.

"Where is it, Mr. D?" yelled Tyler anxiously.

"Where?" echoed Will, shaking his head. "It's gone by now—long gone."

"You sure?" asked Tyler.

"Yes."

"Well," Tyler persisted, "if it were anywhere in the house, where might it be?"

"Tyler, I've just about had enough of you trying to see how late you can stay up," said Will suspiciously.

"No, that's not why I'm asking, Mr. D, honest. I just want to have a look at your Bible...you know, see if it's the same as mine, when I get mine tomorrow." Tyler had an adventurous look in his eye.

"There will be no tomorrow unless I see you in bed in the next ten seconds!"

Tyler smiled, then sprinted for the bed.

"See ya in the mornin'!" he said as he flipped under the covers.

"Yes," said Will with a tight-lipped smile of his own.

He shut off the light and closed the door behind him.

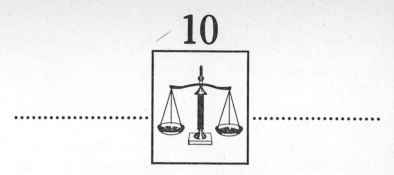

10

The Face Behind the Mask

THE FINAL INTRUSION was almost over.

At least that's what the church bulletin said. This hymn was the final event of today's service, next to the entry entitled "Pastor's Final Comments."

The question in Will's mind was when was the elderly woman who played the organ—who seemed like she was in a world of her own, totally oblivious to the time constraints of any one of the hundreds of worshipers— going to hit the last note of the hymn? It just didn't seem possible that the author of this hymn had actually intended the work to drag out that way. Up and down the scale she went, hitting and holding what seemed, to him, such inappropriate notes.

Will's mind wandered to the massive organ pipes

jutting upward along the wall behind the orchestra section, which was easily able to hold an entire orchestra. Tyler's church was more like an auditorium in size, capable of holding nearly a thousand people. Row after row of pews arched in a semicircle around the pulpit area. There appeared to be a slight downward slant to the floor in order for those in the rear to be able to see what was happening up front. Of course, from where Will and Tyler stood, the slant went the other way. Tyler had insisted that they sit not only near the front, but in the very first row. The boy had mumbled something about hating to look at the back of people's heads when there were some perfectly good seats up front, seats which offered an unobstructed view of the pulpit.

After arriving at Tyler's preferred location, it hadn't taken long for Will to decipher the true purpose of Tyler's insistence. When they had taken their seats, a young man who appeared to be a member of the pastoral staff acknowledged Tyler's presence with a smile. The term "brown noser" came to mind, and a look down at Tyler confirmed Will's hypothesis. Tyler had shrugged, feigning ignorance to his hidden political agenda, but Will had seen through the charade. The kid was no dummy; Will had to admit that much. However, seeing shades of himself in the young boy at his side was not enough to sweeten Will's distaste for where he was or to quell thoughts of the valuable time he was wasting by being here.

Finally, he thought with relief as the organist let the last note build then fade into the stirrings of hundreds of people taking their seats.

A silver-haired man with silver-rimmed glasses walked from a pew that was situated up on the platform near the pulpit. He wore a navy-blue suit, a business suit. There were no visible signs of church ministry in his attire.

This was one part of the service that Will was actually looking forward to, and not because it meant that the service was over. He had surmised that this would be the time that the pastor would speak of the Jesus Trial, as his trial had popularly been labeled.

There was no question, he thought, that this would be the time when the church leader would try to calm his flock, to prepare them for the turmoil ahead for the figurehead of the Christian church. That is, he thought, if this minister had any guts. Will sat back with an inward expression of triumph to listen to the pastor's final comments.

The pastor adjusted his glasses.

"Funny how in a world of wall-to-wall people it is so difficult to get one, just one to listen to your problems," he began, "your concerns, or your dreams. Many of us have a deep need for someone who will listen. Not to just pay you nod service while he or she glances away, but someone who'll *really* listen.

"Few of us realize it, but that someone that many of us long for is with us every moment of every day. He's there when you are in that meeting in your boss's office facing potential termination of your job; He's there at the bedside of your friend who is ill; He's there at the graveside of someone you have lost; and He's there when you accomplish one of your dreams.

"That Person is the Son of God.

"Do you find that hard to believe?" asked the pastor, looking over the congregation. "Because I do—that the Son of God cares enough about my petty problems, about your problems, that He would lower His kingly head to listen to us."

The eloquent pastor paused and leaned closer to the microphone.

"Believe it," he said plainly.

"There is no better time than now to open a dialogue with your living Savior. Especially in this time when sensationalist media events..."

"Ah ha!" said Will under his breath. "There it is!"

"...pass over and through our lives like a great ship over the sea. And in its wake spirals a vortex of swirling water, threatening to sweep you and I into its great downward plunge." Will was lost in his thoughts, so he did not notice the eyes of the man at the pulpit upon him.

"I don't know about you, but at times like these I could use something to keep my head above water. Something that floats no matter what the weight."

The senior pastor laid his notes in the open book on the pulpit.

"To my right is a room marked "Prayer Room." In it are kind men and women trained to do one thing, and that is to listen. If you have a need or question, they are there to listen to you. These people will be here every Sunday for the needs and problems that you have that can wait till the end of the week for someone to listen, but our Savior Jesus Christ is at your side the very second the need arises, and no one listens in quite the same way as He."

The congregation began to gather their things, signaling that the service was over.

Will looked down at Tyler, who was signaling something entirely different. He was signaling to the assistant pastor running the confirmation class to come over and say hello so he could score some more brownie points.

"Hey, Pastor!" Tyler yelled.

The confirmation class met twice a week for six months on Tuesdays and Thursdays with the purpose of preparing the children of the congregation for receiving the bread and wine of communion. During the half year of class, the kids were asked to be at Sunday worship services without fail, which, combined with a Will versus Tyler settlement in Will's study late last night, were the only reasons they were here at all.

But Will's mind had been clicking through the pastor's final comments in the service. A thought had arisen when the silver-haired pastor had made reference to his trial. A thought Will meant to share with the pastor as soon as he was able.

Many in the congregation came up front to shake hands and visit with the senior pastor, and he greeted his flock with pleasant, genuine salutations. Will kept his eye on him and waited for an opening.

The young assistant pastor walked down the steps of the front stage toward the beckons of his eager student. "Tyler," he said, "good to see you! You had the best seat in the house for the service." He playfully tousled Tyler's hair.

"I always sit up front, Pastor Jones," said Tyler. "You know that; you've seen me here every week. I don't like to miss anything."

"No, you don't," said the young man, "and I hope you were paying close attention to Pastor Chuck's sermon, because there will be a quiz on it on Tuesday."

"Did I hear my name mentioned over here somewhere?" Pastor Chuck had broken free from the crowd and was on his way over.

"Hello," he said to Will, offering him his hand. "Chuck Aldrich, if you hadn't guessed, they call me Pastor Chuck around here." The pastor looked to be a man in his late fifties, about the same age as Will.

"Will Dysley, Pastor Aldrich," said Will, shaking the pastor's hand firmly.

"Pastor Jones, Mr. Dysley," said Tyler's instructor, introducing himself.

"Pastor," Will nodded cordially.

"And haven't I seen this young man around?" said Pastor Chuck turning to Tyler.

"Yep, I'm Tyler Hollimon."

"Put it there, Tyler."

"I've been wondering," said Tyler, looking at the sermon notes stuffed into the pastor's Bible. "If you're through with those, I could sure use them!"

Pastor Chuck smiled. "Big quiz Tuesday?" he asked with a chuckle. "Pastor Jones is quite a slave driver, isn't he, Tyler?"

Tyler laughed, but not too loudly. He knew whose hand would be holding the red grading pen.

"Pastor . . . Chuck," Will said with difficulty. "I would like to have a word with you, if I may."

"Certainly, Mr. Dysley," agreed the senior pastor with a knowing look. "Pastor Jones, perhaps you can show Tyler where the new Bibles are."

"They're here!" shouted Tyler, looking excitedly at Will. "And I get one, huh?"

"That's right," Chuck said and nodded at Pastor Jones. "Mr. Dysley and I will be up in a minute."

"All right!" screamed Tyler. He bounded up the aisle weaving around the remaining parishioners, while Assistant Pastor Jones tried to keep up.

"Please," said Pastor Chuck, motioning for Will to have a seat in the first pew. The two men took a seat. "Mr. Dysley," began the silver-haired pastor leaning close to Will, "do you wish to speak of your trial?"

Will's eyes flickered with surprise. Apparently the pastor knew exactly who he was. He quickly regained his focus, as well as his resolve.

"No, Pastor," he said. "I simply wish to comment on a statement that you made."

Pastor Chuck nodded slowly and studied the man next to him.

"You speak as if the media has a corner on sensationalism," said Dysley, "when you and your church are using the greatest hook of all."

The pastor narrowed his eyes and leaned back against the pew.

"Let's set the record straight, Pastor Chuck," said Will firmly with a hint of condescension in his tone. "The only form of mass media involved in creation of a body of knowledge concerning the most entrancing subject of all, namely, life after death, is in print form, and is called the Holy Bible. Certainly you do not consider it to be sensationalist? Yet you condemn the media and our nation's courts for sensationalism from the same pulpit from which you broadcast messages of how a person can achieve immortality." Will sat back with a sarcastic grin.

Pastor Chuck adjusted his glasses and took a minute to gauge what he was truly up against.

"Mr. Dysley," he said with a steady voice, "fear of God is nothing to be ashamed of."

Will noticed a few parishioners were starting to gather around, awaiting their chance to chat with the church leader. He felt the sting of emerging sweat on his forehead.

"Fear?" Will repeated, trying to keep his voice low.

"Yes, fear," confirmed the pastor, his eyes never leaving Will's. "You are obviously not sure you should be handling this case and you are here seeking the blessing of the church. The path you are on has its purpose, Mr. Dysley, or God would not have laid it out for you. You and I speaking here today is by no means an accident; it is assuredly by design.

"Fear," continued the pastor, "is one sure way to come to God."

Will chortled defiantly, reaching into his breast pocket for his pipe. "You see, Pastor, this is exactly why the trial is so necessary, because you're speaking as if you know what you're saying!" Will shook his head and sidled in the pew. Some of the gathered people had taken note of the tension in the air. Will couldn't care less if they were listening.

"Just like you speak as if you know what you're saying about Christ listening intently to our every need, and about the kingdom of heaven awaiting the arrival of the immortal souls of the faithful. It's all based on the sensational, Pastor Chuck—the resurrection of a dead man back to life. And after our last breath, the white light and open arms of the heavenly host welcoming us to paradise.

"The trial is about finally revealing the truth," Will continued, "for all to see. In my line of work, truth is both something to strive for as well as something to be feared. If I choose to ignore it, I am in danger of losing a case. But in your line of work, it's quite the opposite, isn't it? If the truth is revealed you stand to lose your case and more, don't you, Pastor? You stand to lose your eternity.

"So you see," Will chided, "I understand why you choose ignorance over truth, Pastor Chuck; I understand full well."

Just then, the group of people gathered to speak to their senior pastor began to part. Apparently someone was pushing his way through the crowd.

"Check it out!" yelled Tyler, emerging through the wall of dark suits and frilly church dresses.

Will stood and looked down at Tyler, who was happily examining his new Bible. He patted him on the head and thought back to Samantha's words that he might learn something of value by taking Tyler to church, words which turned out to be true. He smiled and turned one last time to the still-seated pastor.

"All miracles and all sensations, including the one on which your life is based, must one day fade away into the black and white of truth," Dysley seethed. "If fear exists in this room, it lives in you, Pastor Chuck, and it is the fear that the charade is up. And isn't it time we all saw if there's a face behind the mask?"

The pastor smiled pleasantly and respectfully stood while Will Dysley walked up the center aisle with Tyler hopping along next to him.

After he had greeted and chatted with the final person in the after-service procession, the silver-haired pastor retired to the privacy of his ready room and asked his Savior to listen to him one more time.

11

Self-Serving Eyes

THE LOW, EARLY-MORNING sun beamed through the multicolored stained-glass windows of the regal old courtroom. The sun's rays inched their way up the massive podium of Judge Alexander as the morning wore on, whitening the dark wood as it went. Clouds of airborne dust twinkled in and out of the strips of light like snowflakes. The media personnel scuffled busily over the government-green tile floor, checking and double-checking their cables and connections on their equipment. Day two of the trial was about to begin, and it was sure to draw a big audience.

In fact, it would later be reported that the circulation of the newspapers following day two, as well as the Nielsen ratings of the TV newscasts, would show marked increases compared with day one of the trial. However, one did not have to puzzle long over the cause of all the commotion, the reason for the sudden increase in reader and viewer interest. It was not every day the mass audience had a chance to witness firsthand the courtroom mastery of the man considered the sharpest legal mind on Earth.

Will Dysley sat patiently at the table along with representatives from the Longview school board and his sharply tailored *Legal Entourage*. Tom Weber appeared anything but relaxed sitting sideways, facing the windows at the far end of the table. He dabbed his forehead periodically, somewhat conscious of how shiny it could become if too much sweat was left to mix with his natural oils.

Across the way sat Randell Clive with the angelic mother-daughter duo of Elizabeth and Mary Magellan next to him. Having delivered before the court what was definitely the most original approach to date concerning the current constitutional ban on religion or prayer in public places, he could only sit quietly and wonder how his one-time schoolmate would answer his argument. He had counted on the element of surprise in preparing his dramatic opening argument, but he knew it was lost in the recent swap of opposing counsel from novice Robert Lapper to Will Dysley. This could only mean that Will Dysley, like himself, had never forgotten his zealous pledge of vengeance. He would know in mere moments if the famous, sharp-tongued attorney would be able to present a plausible argument which would make jurists who, he thought, had to have at least a slight susceptibility to the fear of divine retribution, side with him. If

Will Dysley had retained any of the truculent nature of his youth, and everything about him suggested that he had, Randell Clive knew he would be in for quite a rally.

People around the globe tuned their sets into the action as network news cameras panned the hordes of protesters outside the courthouse. Not only had the TV audience and the newspaper readers grown in number as word of the Jesus Trial seeped under the doors of those less in touch with their world, but the protesters and demonstrators also had multiplied since the opening day of the trial. The estimates reached figures as high as a million, tying the all-time high turnout of a recent rally staged in Washington D.C. by the prolific freedom-of-choicers. "My, oh my!" remarked a much-quoted columnist from a national newspaper. "How religious issues bring 'em out!"

Tom Weber's hopes of a quiet, uneventful retirement flashed before his eyes in nightmarish scenes of cross-wielding Christians in chariots traipsing through his yard. He again wiped the dripping sweat from his brow, forgetting for a moment that he must be in the frames of the several cameras which were undoubtedly trained on his partner at the other end of the table. People were calming down and taking their places, the judge and jury were filing in. *Soon it would all be out in the open,* he thought. *And did Will seem to care?*

A disturbed glance in Will's direction revealed to Weber a man as cold and calculating as the battering wind outside. He watched as his partner showed no trepidation as he stood at the bequest of the honorable Judge Montgomery Alexander.

"Thank you, your Honor," he said respectfully. "Thank you very much, sir."

Although a man in his late fifties, Will Dysley looked quite good. He wore a perfectly tailored, perfectly pressed dark suit, again with a perfectly matched conservative, but not altogether boring tie. He had, as they say, aged gracefully during his long, successful career. What they probably hadn't noticed, however, was that his simply being in front of a judge and jury seemed to peel the years off of him like a youth-replenishing emolient. He made his way efficaciously to the center of the floor, his distinct, pervasive eyes filling the TV screens in the homes of America with clear direction.

"You and I have been placed in an awkward, perhaps terrible position," he began, his voice clear but intoned with empathy. "My opponent," he said pointing to the table where his old schoolmate sat, "has put us there. He has forced this upon us, as much as you and I wanted to let it lie." His voice held a touch of reluctance and a feeling that he was confiding in the listener, like a president in a fireside chat before he unilaterally decides to destroy the world.

"What's done is done, however," he said sadly, "and now we must find a reason for what we've been forced to do. You and I together must try to justify the action forced upon us."

Will bowed his head in mock homage. "And that action forced upon us is to dive headfirst into a story that has been a part of our lives for many generations—a story that many of us consider sacred. How, you may ask, can we justify defiling this story?" Will asked. "How can we participate in what many both inside and outside these walls consider to be a sacrilegious act?"

Tom Weber watched as his partner masterfully tried to put the jury in their corner. As many times as he had watched his partner perform over the years, it never ceased to amaze him. It was something he just couldn't get out of his head—the pure ease with which he forged his arguments and the eloquent way he delivered them. As well as he knew Will Dysley the man, it was still very difficult not to put him on a pedestal. It was still difficult not imagining his every word spilling straight from his mouth onto the stark white pages of legal history.

"The reason, my friends," Will continued, smiling slightly and slowly making his way over to the jury box, "is very clear. In fact, it is crystal clear. It is a reason tied to a human right as basic as the right to breathe the air. It is, in fact, a natural right tied to the very reason this court was created." Will careened his head around, looking at the impressive grandeur of the old courtroom.

"It is, men and women of the jury, our right to know the truth."

Will took care to hold the jury's attention by using what Dysley considered a precious natural resource—that is, unidirectional, unwavering eye contact.

"You and I have earned the right to understand the things which influence our lives," he continued forcibly, "to test them by our most reliable means. Even if some of those things have remained shielded in the cloak of religious tradition all these years.

"The resurrection of Christ is a myth that has greatly affected the lives of people over the past two thousand years, and the controversy seems to now be coming to a head. The battles rage in our courts as well as in our communities over whether to allow nativity scenes in public places at Christmastime, or whether a cross and scepter may adorn a city emblem on the doors of police cars and at the top of government letterhead without offending someone, or if officials can wear jewelry in the shape of a cross at a city council meeting, or whether to teach evolution or creation to our children in our schools.

"And here, in this case," he emphasized, "whether our children should be allowed to pray in school. And all because of this one, single myth laying dormant in the enshrouding fog of religious dogma.

"How far does it have to go before we demand the truth?" Dysley declaimed. "How much does it need to affect our day-to-day lives before we claim our right to know? And, I ask you," he added, "can it ever be sacrilege to seek truth?"

Tom Weber felt the tide of sentiment rising; the people in the courtroom were buying it. Everyone in the world, it seemed, was starting to agree with his eloquent partner. They too were undeniably tired of the recurring theme of prayer in schools pervading the nation's courts at every level for the past three decades. Truth, he felt them agreeing, would surely put an end to the controversy once and for all.

"Much lesser public issues," Will continued, "which have affected our lives to a much lesser degree have even caught our attention long enough so that we sought the truth. The impact of this two-thousand-year-old myth cannot be denied, and we, the American people, can no longer turn our backs on a myth which the opposing counsel would use to open the floodgates of our schools to religion and prayer.

"This case, as you can see, was unavoidable and inevitable. It, like every other issue which affects our lives, must be put to the test—however sacred or untouchable it may be. And that is exactly what I intend to do."

Will walked casually to his table. He picked up a thick book and flapped it back and forth on its binder. "In pretrial hearings," he said with a smile, "I elected without a fight to allow the words of this book to be viewed by this court as factual evidence."

He looked at the book and flashed a brighter smile. "No, you didn't miss your guess; it's the Bible all right, and the holy one at that." There were a few chuckles in the back of the courtroom. One of the secondary-action media cameras whirled around to capture it for the evening news.

"It is the book from which the counsel for the plaintiff will draw his conclusions and I want you to accept it as you would any eyewitness testimony." Will paused and studied the reaction of the jury. The jurists were shifting in their seats, unable to fathom the rationale behind Dysley's move to accept the Bible as valid evidence. How could he do that, they thought, and still hope to win?

"Puzzled?" he asked. "Shocked?"

Will tapped the leather cover of the book.

"Well," he said a little sadly, "this is all we have to go

on." Will examined the book closely. "This is all the opposing counselor has on which to base his arguments; it is his only source of evidence, his only source of proof. It is filled with words written, some believe, through divine intervention by men who actually claimed to feel the presence of God as they wrote. Now, I am not so haughty as to expect to challenge the existence of God with my argument; that would be ludicrous," Will admitted and then paused.

"It is, rather, man's reliability which is in question in this trial, not God's," he said with conviction. "And it is the all-too-human authors of this text that will serve as the litmus test for that reliability."

Will set down the Bible and walked back out to the center of the floor. "I admit that the premise of my argument," he said, "like that of my opponent, will be mere speculation because the Bible is all that remains after two thousand years, yet I will introduce one major difference."

Will paused and walked slowly until he reached the table of the opposing counsel. He looked intently at Randell Clive, and said, "Whereas my opponent's case will be rooted in the unknown—in that which is mysterious, that which is miraculous—mine will be rooted in the established patterns of human nature, patterns we've all come to know painfully well." Will turned to face the jury.

"In order to win his case, my opponent would have you accept the resurrection of a dead man back to life," he said. "A miracle in its truest form. A miracle that to this day our greatest scientific minds have been unable to duplicate. And he would have us accept this miracle as fact. I, on the other hand, will ask you to do nothing of the sort. I will ask you to do nothing more than to turn to your right or to your left and witness the common humanity of your neighbor." Will returned to his table and lifted another book. He opened it to a premarked page.

"Perhaps David Hume, an eighteenth-century philosopher known for his skepticism, put it best when he said:

> There is not to be found in all of history any miracle attested by a sufficient number of men, of such unquestioned good sense, education, and learning, as to secure us against all delusions in themselves.[1]

Will read the quote again, this time even more imperatively, to be sure no one missed it. He closed the book with a chuckle.

"Skeptic though he may have been," he said, "you have to admit, the man has a point. Given what we know about ourselves, we do not have to look hard to find our dirty human fingers at the roots of an alleged miracle. We have all learned through the tough realities of life that miracles are for Disneyland fairy tales, and if a miracle was alleged to have taken place, human deception cannot be far away.

"I submit and intend to prove that the alleged miracle of the resurrection of Jesus Christ was no different."

Will walked slowly to the center of the courtroom

floor, knowing full well that the self-serving eyes of the world were upon him.

"And I think we deserve to know the truth," he said. "Don't you?"

12

So Help Me, God

RANDELL CLIVE GULPED hard after having just been treated to a dose of extremely skillful rebuttal. It was perhaps the best and most plausible way to refute the opening argument he had presented earlier in the trial. Although he wasn't completely sure where Dysley was going with his counterargument, it was, nevertheless, definitely too late to make any major adjustments in the agenda he had slated for this morning. He rose somewhat reluctantly to address the judge and to call his first witness.

"Mr. Clive," said Judge Alexander in a startling, scruffy burst of voice, halting Clive in midstride. "Before you call your first witness, sir, we have one other matter."

The decrepit judge leafed through the stack of papers

next to him searching, it seemed, for something in particular. It was indeed rare for Judge Alexander to be the cause for any form of delay in his courtroom. He was the type of judge who wanted to get them in and out as quickly as possible with the least amount of tangential interruption. He liked to listen to the arguments, review them briefly in the privacy of his chambers, and in mere minutes emerge with a judgment. Those who were acquainted with him knew this must be something forced upon him by some higher authority. And, to quote from that particular higher authority:

> *Given the confused and prodigious nature of this case which has served to discombobulate the U.S. trial court system in sort of a disestablishmentarianistic manner, we, the Supreme Court of the land, are making adjustments in established procedures in an attempt to maintain fairness.*

Judge Alexander was alternately raising his eyebrows, then knitting them together, straining to read the wordy memo handed down from the Supreme Court after their pretrial review and approval of the arguments. He was trying to find a logical break in the forty-page memo so he could read the important stuff aloud, but it was written so as to make it all seem important, which it wasn't. He looked over his bifocals, then through them, and it appeared to the people in the audience and at home as if neither way was working very well.

Everyone in the courtroom waited patiently, wondering if there truly came a time in the aging process when nothing could help the deterioration of the eyesight and the other senses, or if it was just a meaningless ritual unique to judges and other stately gents who wanted more time to look for whatever they were looking for, or more time to decide what they were going to say. Only the stately gents, it seemed, knew for sure; and they weren't telling, at least not in a timely manner.

Media managers had grandiose thoughts of using shots of the old judge in a stunning example of inaction in order to build suspense in their presentation of the event, but those thoughts were quickly dismissed and replaced with images of the expensive footage ending up on the cutting-room floor.

"Ahhumm," the judge cleared the buildup of phlegm that seemed perpetually lodged in his throat. He muttered something to himself. "The uh, Supreme Court of the United States had one other adjustment in the due process of law in Magellan versus Longview Elementary," he said, flipping back and forth through the thick memo. "Has to do with the swearing in of witnesses to the stand. I've been asked to read this aloud." And he read:

> There is, we believe, grounds for contradiction between certain language in the witness oath and the arguments to be presented by counsel, sufficient to alter that oath for the duration of the trial. The oath assumes the existence of a supernatural being for which there is no material proof recognized by this court, a being who is capable of miraculous acts akin to the one in question in the case. It

is, therefore, inappropriate to lend credence to said supernatural being giving him jurisdiction over the authenticity and validity of testimony. The language, specifically, 'So help me, God,' is hereby stricken from the witness oath in the case of Magellan versus Longview Elementary.

Judge Alexander raised his eyebrows and looked over his bifocals at the counsel for the plaintiff.

"All right, Mr. Clive," he said with an exhausted wave of his hand. "Proceed."

Two sets of big blue eyes belonging to Elizabeth and Mary Magellan watched as Clive resumed his walk to the center of the floor.

"The prosecution calls Dr. Eldon Jonas," Clive announced.

The bailiff, trying to look as authoritative and as legal as possible for the cameras, led the witness to the stand.

Dr. Eldon Jonas looked like he had come straight off a South Carolina porch where he sat all day with a pitcher of lemonade and a group of his slow-moving peers philosophizing about life. One could imagine him blending in with the weeping willows along a slow-moving riverbed town in the Deep South. He wore a summer-weight straw hat that had somehow survived the blustery winds outside. He sported a totally inappropriate white suit, given the season, with light blue pinstripes. His mustache composed of coarse strands of hair, as unusual as it might seem, mirrored the bluish-white colors of the suit.

He removed his hat as the bailiff reached for the witness-oath Bible, looked at the judge, then stopped himself. The bailiff was doing a tremendously bad job of smoothing over the missing part of trial procedure. He stumbled on a step as he led Doctor Eldon Jonas to the stand, chagrined that he had forgotten to do his job correctly.

"Dr. Jonas," Clive said, sauntering toward his witness, "thank you for coming today, sir." Clive nodded respectfully. "Doctor, in your forty-five years as curator of the Religious Archives Department at the Smithsonian Institute, and in the twenty years that you've chaired the World Conference on Biblical Authenticity," he said somewhat thrasonically, "you have undoubtedly come across quite a few variations in the story of the resurrection?"

Dr. Jonas leaned on his left elbow while toying with the tips of his mustache.

"Yessir," he answered with a distinct, back-of-the-throat, southern-born pitch. "Many, many stories, sir."

Clive came closer to the witness stand.

"For the benefit of some of us here, Doctor, I'd like to ask you to relay to us what you feel is the most accurate historical interpretation of the facts, starting..."

"Objection!" boomed Tom Weber, releasing quite a blast of pent-up anxiety. "None of this is historical, and none of this is fact. That's what we're here to determine, your Honor."

Tom looked over at his partner, who hadn't yet reacted to his undiscussed objection. Tom knew that this was Will's trial and that he probably wouldn't react favorably to his outburst, but the law firm whose abilities and reputation was under the macroscope of the world was his baby as well. This, he thought, gave him the right to object. Will Dysley sat quietly, studying the judge.

"Sustained," said the judge, after a moment of thought. Whenever Judge Alexander addressed attorneys or witnesses, it seemed such a bother to him that his tone was always initially belligerent, but then it usually eased up a bit. He pointed his finger limply at Randell Clive.

"You there, Mr. Clive," he said. "Refrain from any further assumptive language. The jury will not accept the witness's recounting of the story as historical fact, but merely as conjecture. Proceed, Counselor."

"Dr. Jonas," Clive began anew with a clever smirk, "if you would, please tell us the most *widely accepted* story of what occurred starting after Jesus was sentenced to be crucified by Pontius Pilate, the Roman procurator."

"After the sentencin'?" Dr. Jonas said with an exaggerated, inquisitive look. "Well, sir, there were certain rituals the accused had ta go through, atrocious rituals that fall'ed the sentencin'. The first a' which was to tie the accused to a post in a public area, strip 'im of his clothes, and whip 'im!"

Jonas was acting out his words, emphasizing them with descriptive movements. Tying, stripping, and whipping. He adjusted the sleeves of his suit, which had ridden up his arms after his acting out the curling back of a whip and slashing it forward.

"Now, the whip," Jonas said with a curious grin, the kind you get when you're telling people something you know they would rather not hear, "was an instr'ment of nightmarish proportions itself, Mr. Clive. It was a strip a' leather 'bout yea wide, with shards a' dried bone an' sharp stones embedded in it. It was called a flag'rum.

"See," he continued, scooting to the edge of his chair to further free up his arms, "the Jews limited their whippers to forty lashes, but them Romans had no limit. Christ was sentenced by the Romans, so all's that was left a' him after they were through was ribbons a' flesh dangling from his shoulders, his bowels torn an' layin' open fer public viewin'."

"Is this necessary!" Weber screamed, infuriated. He gave Will a death look of disbelief that he had let this go on as long as it had. Couldn't Will see the damage this was doing? Didn't Will know that scenes of torture usually elicit sympathy from people? Will remained unmoved and untroubled.

"It is very necessary, your Honor," insisted Clive. "I am merely in the process of dispelling potential arguments by the defense, which may be the reason the defense is objecting so vigorously," he added cleverly. "The conclusion of this line of questioning will be instrumental to my case, your Honor."

"Witness will continue," said the judge, who seemed too enthralled with the testimony of the witness to stop him now. He had never known about the precrucifixion rituals in the time of Christ.

Dr. Jonas pushed up his sleeves, preparing for his next round of gestures.

"Now, Christ survived the whippin', so he grad'iated ta the next level a' punishment. The Roman guards had heard that Christ had been called the King o' the Jews, so they made a crown a' thorns and mashed it down on his head good an' tight. They threw an ol' purple cape round 'im, an' led 'im through the city ta the site a' the crucifixion.

"There they laid Christ down ov'r a large wooden cross and drove iron spikes about an inch across through his wrists about here," Jonas showed the jury, "an' through his heels down here pinning 'im ta the cross." The southern-born doctor of archaeology was still acting out his words and phrases in exaggerated movements. It would have been comical to the people of the jury and the people gathered in the courtroom as well as the viewers at home had they not been so appalled at what he was saying. "Then they raised 'im upright an' dug the cross into the ground."

"What caused him to die, Doctor?" asked Clive.

Those people inescapably present in the court were shocked into silence. Elizabeth turned to her daughter to make sure the headset gently playing nursery rhymes in her ears was still on securely. Clive had warned her of the strength of the first witness's testimony and obtained a court-approved allowance to protect his young client. Little Mary bounced her feet and softly sung the words she knew of the nursery songs, oblivious to the harsh goings on.

"Well," said Jonas contemplatively, "I ain't no medical doctor, but I've been told what'd happen to a man hangin' on a cross fer a peri'd a' time." Dr. Jonas raised his arms to shoulder level.

"The arms," he explained, "would grow tir'd. Air could be drawn inta the lungs, but not exhaled. Carbon dioxi'd would build up in the lungs and in the bloodstream; circulation would be insufficient to feed the heart an' the brain. Christ either died a' suffication, bein' unable to exhale the air from his lungs, or from heart failure."

"Did anyone check to make sure he was dead?" asked Clive.

"The guards, yessir. The Roman guards made sure of it."

"How did they do that, Doctor?"

"With a spear. They thrust a spear in his side, you see. Blood and water came spillin' out."

"What does that tell us, Doctor?"

"Well, if you know yer physiology, the blood was there 'cause his heart had ruptured and the water was most likely pericard'l fluid from the sac 'round the heart. It is a clear liquid like water. The spear a' the guards confirmed that Christ's heart must a' burst somewhere along the line."

Randell Clive gave time for the ensuing silence to infiltrate its intended targets. There was a lot of uncomfortable shifting among the jurists and the courtroom audience. The networks, however, had prepared well for just such a sensational possibility. They began splitscreening the harsh testimony with artistic renditions of the horrors of crucifixion. As liberally contradictory as this testimony was, the networks simply couldn't pass up a chance like this to boost ratings by giving the people what they wanted; namely, death graphically illustrated in its most hideous form.

"Please continue, Doctor."

Doctor Eldon Jonas was the only one in the courtroom who appeared to be at complete ease with the subject matter he was discussing. He and Will Dysley, that is, who sat in deep concentration, his percipient eyes trained on the witness as he spoke.

"Christ was taken down from the cross," Jonas continued, "and given to a wealthy Jew named Joseph a' Arimathea, who had petitioned Pilate fer the body. As was the custom, the body was cleansed and wrapped in spices. Myrrh and aloes mainly, the weight of which was supposed ta correspond ta the stature of the deceased. Christ was wrapped, I b'lieve, in about a hundr'd pounds a' spices and laid in Joseph's donated tomb outside a' the city."

"And that first Easter morning?" Clive asked.

"Well, history says..." Jonas looked sheepishly at Judge Alexander. "Sorry, your Honor. The *story* goes," he corrected himself with a smile, "that the reason ol' Joseph a' Arimathea was so willin' to give Jesus one a' his tombs, was 'cause he knew he'd only need it fer the weekend!" Jonas let out a yelp of laughter and gave his knee a sharp slap.

A scintilla of disapproving laughter trickled across a scattered few members of the courtroom audience who understood Dr. Jonas's somewhat ill-timed joke. "'Cause," the doctor continued, recovering the seriousness in his tone, "in three days, the tomb was found empty, the body missin'. Christ was gone."

"And who discovered the empty tomb, Doctor?" Clive asked.

"Mary Magdalene, Mary the wife of Clopas, an' another woman named Salome. When they arrived at the tomb, they found the boulder that had been used ta block the entrance was rolled away. When they entered the tomb, they found the burial cloth lyin' on the floor. The body a' Jesus weren't there."

Randell Clive walked away from the witness stand toward the jury.

"I am sorry," he said, "to have put you all through this grueling description of the events surrounding the story of the resurrection, but the defense would have most certainly challenged the fact that Christ was actually dead when he was laid in the tomb.

"There are many who believe that he wasn't dead and that he crawled from the tomb and disappeared forever, thereby assuring his name would reach mythical stature. We have heard from Dr. Jonas, as close as we can come to an expert witness, that this was not possible. And given what we've heard of the hideous abuses associated with the sentencing of an individual to crucifixion, I think we have to conclude that it would have been more of a miracle for Christ to have survived the horrors he was subjected to by his executioners than for him to be resurrected from the dead."

Clive placed his hands on the jury box railing.

"A dead body was laid in that tomb, a very dead body," he said. "A dead body that had somehow rolled away a massive boulder and crawled away through the desert leaving an empty tomb for the proliferation of a religion which even today, spans the entire world.

"Seems kind of ridiculous to entertain such a notion, doesn't it?"

Clive walked back to his table. He smiled and took the earphones off of his young client.

"Nothing further, your Honor," he said, glancing over at the opposing counsel.

13

Deficient Minds and Inferior Intellects

TOM WEBER looked worried.

What a terribly masterful way for Clive to begin the trial, he thought. He had simply followed the textbook method of argument in murder cases: show the jury the victim lying helpless in a pool of blood and trigger a sympathetic response. But this particular victim was no ordinary person; this victim was considered by some to be the Son of God. The jury, he knew, was eating it up.

As justification for the extremity of his expert witness's testimony, Clive had used the premise that he needed to dispel any notions that the jury may have had that Christ had survived the crucifixion and, therefore, been able to walk away from the whole mess, and thus fulfill his promise. Clive had gotten away with it beautifully; no one suspected a thing. They were all too shocked, Weber thought hopelessly.

He saw no way out of this one. And that is precisely why cases like this involving intense cross-examinations of hostile witnesses were left to the other founding partner in the firm of Dysley, Weber, & Associates. No matter how well-coached the witness was, no matter how well-versed he was in the potentially devastating lines of questioning and how to avoid them, Will Dysley always seemed to find a way in.

In a recent article, a legal journal attempted to define the way Will analyzed the arguments of the opposing counsel:

> ... Dysley seems to be almost computerlike in his processing of data during the arguments of opposing counsels. He studies each argument as if it is a three-dimensional holographic image, turning it in his mind and viewing it at every angle, until a flaw in design or an entryway is revealed. Then he attacks, leaving only the disintegrating remnants of truth lingering in the minds of the jurists.

Will Dysley stood with authority, pulling his suit coat tight by the lapels.

"Dr. Jonas," he said, striding toward the witness, his heels clicking loudly on the tile floor. "In your research, I am certain that you have come across a description of a military detail known as a Roman guard unit."

"Yessir," said Jonas, nodding.

"Will you kindly tell us what it was?" said Dysley, arriving at the witness stand.

"I will, sir," he said. And, as the folks at home and the courtroom audience had come to expect, the southern-born doctor raised his hands and shoulders, which seemed to be a prerequisite any time he planned on opening his mouth. They hoped that this next description, with full gesturing accompaniment, would be a little more palatable than the last.

"The Roman guard unit was a highly trained, highly disciplined military unit," he said with the spirit of a true military man. "The unit consisted a' eight ta sixteen men, I b'lieve. The Romans used the unit ta protect a piece a' land from any an' all comers. The men would line up four on each side of a square. They were told ta hold that square, whatever the cost."

"And if they failed, Doctor?" Will asked tersely.

"Failure?" said Jonas abruptly. "No such thing as a second chance in those ranks, sir, no such thing. All failures suffered incredible incentive-inducin' forms a' dyin'!" Some in the audience who had caught on to Dr. Jonas's odd humorous comment laughed softly.

"Like what, Dr. Jonas?" Dysley continued with a slight grin, as if he were sharing Jonas's joke. His grin, however, was for a greater cleverness of his own making.

"Like, bein' burned alive in a fire started with a pile a' yer own clothes!" exclaimed the doctor. "How's that fer incentive?"

"Very persuasive," said Will as he walked to the other side of the witness stand. "Doctor," he continued, "is there a record of a Roman guard unit being dispatched to the tomb of Christ?"

Doctor Jonas twirled his mustache. "Yessir, there most definitely is."

"Well, Doctor," said Will, starting to rock back and forth on his heels with his arms clasped behind him. The click of his heels echoed above the droning hum of the cameras in the corners. "The Romans must have been protecting something valuable at the tomb of Christ. Do you happen to know what it was?"

"'A' course I do!" yelled the old scholar. "Pilate sent the guard ta prevent the body from disappearin' on 'em!"

Click...click went Will's heels in perfect cadence.

"Doctor Jonas," he said, pausing to look out at the courtroom audience, "are you suggesting that the Roman authorities actually knew about the promise Christ made to rise from the grave in three days?" Click...click.

"Why yes, they knew, Counselor!" shouted Jonas, waving his fist. "Why do ya think Pilate sent the guard?"

"OK Doctor, calm down now," said Will soothingly. "I have a couple more questions and I promise they won't be so elementary. How did the Roman authorities find out about the promise Christ made?" Click... click, Will swayed rhythmically.

"I thought you said no more element'ry questions?" inquired the doctor, looking a little sickeningly at Counselor Clive seated at his table. He was obviously feeling uncomfortable, unable to determine the purpose of this line of questioning.

Dr. Jonas, however, was not alone. No one in the courtroom knew where the world's most logical mind was taking them.

Click... click... click.

Will looked to Judge Alexander for assistance.

"Answer the questions, witness," said the judge plainly.

Dr. Jonas complied. "How'd they know 'bout the promise?" he repeated. "Jesus had said what he planned ta do many times throughout his journeys."

Click! Will's heels jarred the tile floor in a final, exaggerated noise. "Can you repeat that, Dr. Jonas?" he said, turning one ear toward the witness.

"What's that, sir? You mean that Jesus told ev'r'one what he was gonna do?"

Dysley nodded.

"You want verses?"

"If it is convenient."

Dr. Jonas thought for a moment.

"Well, I suppose the first mention was in the early part a' John," he said while looking at the ceiling. "'Round chapter two, verse nineteen, I b'lieve. When Christ and his disciples overturned the tables of the money-changers in the temple.

"The Jews asked Christ why he had destroyed things in the temple, an' Christ answered, 'Destroy this temple an' I'll raise it up in three days.' He was referring ta the resurrection." Jonas tapped his chin.

Will made his way back to his table.

"Then Christ made a direct reference ta what was ta happen ta 'im in Luke nine, verse twenty-two, when he said, 'The Son a' Man must suffa' many things, and be rejected by the elders an' chief priests an' scribes, and be killed, and be raised the third day.'"

Dysley was flipping pages to premarked tabs in the Bible that he had on the table, as if he was following along.

"And again after Christ healed the lepers in Galilee," Jonas continued. "Luke, I b'lieve, Luke eighteen, verses thirty-one ta thirty-three, where Jesus pulled the disciples aside and said..." Jonas cleared his throat and quoted the words of Christ, "'Behold, we are goin' up ta Jerusalem, and all things that are written by the prophets concerning the Son a' Man will be accomplished. For he will be deliva'd ta the Gentiles, an' will be mocked, an' insulted, an' spit upon. And they'll scourge an' put 'im to death. And the third day he'll rise again.'"

Jonas flattened his mustache with his forefinger. He searched his memory for a minute.

"And at the Last Supper," Dysley blurted out as he stooped over the open Bible on the table. "To name yet another time the promise was revealed, Doctor. Jesus told the disciples that they would not see him in a little while. But after a little while they would. He meant that he was going to die then come back and see them afterwards, didn't he, Doctor?"

"Yessir, that is what Christ meant."

Will closed the Bible but kept it in his hand as he walked back toward the witness. "Let me ask you," he said, "does the Bible make any mention of a plot by the disciples to sort of help this promise of Christ's along a little?"

Jonas looked puzzled. "I'm not sure I follow?" he said.

"Well, Doctor," said Will, "certainly the disciples knew what fools they would appear to be if Christ's promise didn't come true. They would be exposed as fools following a false prophet. My question is, does the text mention any attempt the disciples might have made to make sure Christ's body was indeed gone that third day, just like he had told them it would be so many times throughout their journeys?

"Does it mention if there were any attempts by the disciples to make sure the tomb was empty three days after Christ's body was laid in it? Perhaps some attempt by the disciples to steal the body, or—"

"Impossible!" yelled Dr. Jonas, agitated. "That is the same excuse for the empty tomb that the Romans tried to spread throughout Jerusalem! It is complete lunacy fer two reasons," argued Jonas.

"One, the disciples were no match fer the Roman guard unit Pilate sent to guard the tomb. They'd a' been eaten alive by them boys. And two, they didn't understand 'bout the promise."

Dysley came close to the witness. "What did you say, Doctor?"

"I said the disciples didn't understand 'bout Christ's promise ta rise in three days, so why would they have tried ta steal the body?"

Dysley looked with shock at the jury. He walked toward them.

"They didn't understand?" he said over his shoulder. "But Dr. Jonas, the verses you so eloquently recited—" Will seemed confused. "I thought you said Christ told the disciples repeatedly about his promise?"

"Well, yessir," said Jonas a little uncertainly.

"Then how could they *not* understand, Doctor?"

"Well..." said Jonas, hesitating. "Scripture says...," Jonas searched his mind. "It says that Christ's words were hidden from them."

"Hidden from them?" said Dysley, bewildered. "By whom?"

Jonas paused for a long minute. Dysley waited in the wings like a shark keeping his distance after he has made a killing strike so as not to be injured by the thrashings of the dying prey.

"The Bible really don't say," Jonas admitted.

Randell Clive put his hand over his face.

"It doesn't seem to have been hidden from Pilate and the Romans, does it, Doctor?" Will pointed out. "They sent their army's most highly trained military unit to make sure Christ's promise did not come true. Isn't that right, Dr. Jonas?"

"Yessir...," said Jonas dejectedly.

The master orator walked the length of the court-room, the media cameras following like a pack of stray dogs after you've made the mistake of feeding them. Will, however, did not seem to mind. He was exactly where he wanted to be. Exactly.

"Let's get this straight now, Doctor," he said as he paced. "Pilate was intelligent enough to send a guard unit to the tomb where the body of Christ was laid because he had heard whisperings that Christ had made a promise to rise from the tomb. And that promise held a potential threat to the Roman Empire if it were to come true—a real threat to the monocratic rule which recognized one ultimate king, one ultimate ruler, namely, Caesar.

"Yet the very disciples of Christ, who ate with Jesus, who slept under the stars with him, who followed him for years, and who were told directly of his promise to rise from the dead in three days, did not understand!"

Randell Clive sunk a little in his chair.

Will walked until he was in front of the jury.

"You're telling us they did not comprehend, Doctor?" he said loudly.

He walked until he was in front of the judge.

"That they did not get his point?" he said incredulously.

He walked until he was in front of the courtroom audience.

"You're telling us that the disciples didn't understand?" he repeated. "That they just somehow missed the boat?"

Will walked back to face the old scholar. "Dr. Jonas," he said, "have you any reason *why* these men who followed Christ didn't understand about the promise?"

Jonas shook his head sullenly.

Will turned to the jury, studying the Bible in his hands. "Are we to believe the words that I've taken straight out of this text?" he said, tapping the cover. "A text which I so graciously allowed to be accepted as uncontested fact in this courtroom?"

He paused for a minute, slowly pacing the length of the jury box.

"Because if we are to believe these words," he said, "we must also believe that we are dealing with authors of the text who are, sadly, incompetent. Authors who could not comprehend words spoken clearly to them by the man whose every word they should have been hanging on, a man they thought to be the Messiah.

"Words that somehow found their way to the ears of a Roman leader named Pontius Pilate, who placed enough weight on them to put a military guard unit at the tomb of a man who should not have needed any guarding. Because he was," Will pointed at Clive, "as the opposing counsel and his witness so graphically illustrated for us, very much dead."

Will looked again at the Bible in his hands. "Are we to accept anything written by these men who were clearly of deficient minds and inferior intellect? Or are we to dismiss them and their miraculous story as the myth that it is?"

Dysley returned to his seat at the table.

And, for the first time since the mention of his firm's involvement in this most controversial case, his partner Tom Weber smiled.

14

The Craftsman or the Magician

THE WORLD'S GREATEST legal mind sat alone in his office, puffing lightly on his pipe and watching dusk fall on the Chicago skyline. He wasn't so much relishing his victory in battle from that morning as he was contemplating the upcoming war—a war which the act of waging alone would assure a place in the world's history books but which the winning, he knew, would mean certain immortality for him and his firm.

Even great men visualize applause and adulation in the midst of daydreams, the black robe of an honorary doctorate flowing back behind them as they walk to the podium, the headlines of their accomplishments emblazoned in large bold type across a page. No man is beyond these images.

Will Dysley, however, had tasted sweet victory many

times in his distinguished career, and had learned to temper the distracting, premature thoughts of the spoils of war. Nevertheless, he had waited a long time to fulfill what began as the cocky, reach-for-the-stars goal of a sagacious young law-school graduate: a goal which had slowly evolved through perceived wisdom, arrogance, and impenitent achievement until it was brought down like a soaring eagle from its high flight to within the reach of reality.

He had planted a seed that day, twenty-five years ago—a seed borne from a dead winter glade in the back areas of his mind. The seed's hooked claws had grabbed hold of the bootstraps of a passing thought purposely sloughing its way through an uncharted field of his mind. The willing carrier and the seed had formed an unspoken synergistic alliance, feeding off one another and plotting how they might bring down the eagle.

In a classroom of his youth, the carrier and the seed hit pay dirt in the mind of Randell Clive. The seed, viciously planted in its new ignorant host, found a strong foothold in the dank soil and tenebrous entanglements of the lower mind, where hatred and embarrassment and vengeance make their nest. There they were protected from the light, sheltered by the high canopy and the overgrowth. And now, after twenty-five years of nurturing, the seed had sprouted into a hardened sinewy vine, ready to penetrate the overgrowth and enter the world of light, stretching high enough into the heavens where the soaring eagle was within its reach.

The thoughts raging through Will's mind matched the cold velocity of the persistent wind whipping around outside. His arrogant wanderings were interrupted by the high-pitched voice of his secretary announcing the arrival of his next appointment.

"Professor Renshaw is here to see you, Mr. Dysley," she said, swinging open the door then disappearing.

Will swiveled forward and stood. "Send him in, Gladys," he said as he walked toward the door.

Professor Rubin Renshaw appeared in the light of the open doorway wearing a flat-black overcoat and an olive-colored fedora. He was hunched over from age and cradling a stack of books under his arm. His polished mahogany cane was hooked around his forearm.

"Good evening, sir," he said graciously, tipping his hat.

"Glad you could make it, Professor," said Will, offering his hand to the old scholar. "This wind is keeping a lot of people at home these days. The good news is that they're home watching the trial!"

"Yes, I suppose they would be," said Professor Renshaw, unhooking the cane from his arm. "Interesting stuff, this trial."

"Please," said Will, directing the aged professor to an area just to the side of his desk where three plush, black-leather lounge chairs and a glass coffee table stood next to the impressive expanse of windows.

Renshaw leaned hard on his cane as he followed. He took in the clear signs of ostentation with an unnoticed nod and picked the chair which faced the window and the panoramic view of the city.

Unlike the visitors' chairs directly in front of the desk, the chairs in the lounge area of Dysley's office actually had normal-sized legs on them. The short-legged chairs were reserved for guests over which Dysley desired a psychological edge. Like an animal, his philosophy went, a man looked down upon immediately assumes a subordinate position in the hierarchy, giving him the dominant hand. By placing short-legged chairs in front of his desk, Dysley was able to achieve this effect rather nicely.

However, Dysley determined that this particular guest might not be able to get to his feet after plopping down in such a low-lying chair. He didn't know exactly how old Professor Rubin Renshaw was, but he could guess from the leathery, deep-creviced appearance of his face that this man had seen a lot of history.

Renshaw slowly removed his overcoat and laid it across the back of the chair, and hooked his cane around the chair's puffy arm.

Will went back to his desk and took his pipe from a circular purple-glass ashtray with a cork knob in the center. He banged his pipe against the cork, loosening the black, charred remnants of burned-out tobacco. He flipped open a wooden box that was probably meant for cigars but which he used for storing loose tobacco. He grasped a small wad and crushed it into the bowl of his pipe.

"I watched your performance this morning," said Renshaw before Will had a chance to reveal the purpose of the meeting. His voice was scratchy and deep, and a bit sad, like that of a war-drama narrator. "Very impressive logic, Mr. Dysley; impressive indeed."

Renshaw sat down, placing on his lap the books he was carrying. He removed his hat and lay it gently on top of the stack. He waited while Will struck a match and held it over the bowl of his pipe. He worked the flame in a slow circle around the bowl, evenly lighting the fresh tobacco.

"And that's precisely the reason I asked you here, Professor," said Dysley, blowing out the match with a stream of gray smoke. "Given the line of defensive argument I've chosen for the trial, I need to know if you feel comfortable taking the stand tomorrow. If you find it to be too contradictory to your beliefs," he said nonchalantly, "I can ask one of your colleagues to take the stand. The responses I need are very simple."

"Oh no," said Renshaw with a jovial wave of his hand. "I will take the witness stand. It's not every day I get asked to publicly defame and discredit the men and women in the discipleship of Christ." He smiled assuredly.

"However, you must understand, Mr. Dysley," he turned solemn, leaning forward, "if I didn't believe God had a hand in this trial, I would not be here. That is what prevented my exit that first day in the conference room."

"Yes, yes," said Dysley flippantly. He stood abruptly and moved out from behind his desk. "And the path I'm on has its godly purpose, and our speaking right now is by no means an accident—you sound very much like a pastor I just met." He took another slow draw on his pipe and looked down at Renshaw.

"You still don't understand the significance of this case, do you, Professor?"

Renshaw sat back in the chair. "No," he said, grabbing his cane, "maybe you can enlighten me." He looked up at

Dysley, whose black outline was silhouetted against the evening sky.

"You may not know it," Will said loftily, "but we are *world changers,* Mr. Renshaw, world changers you and I. We are part of the first attempt in the history of mankind to legitimatize a story from the spiritual world by human standards. Never in the history of man has an event like the resurrection been brought before a public system of judgment so it could be rejected or validated by the accepted means."

Will paused to stare out over the Chicago skyline.

Professor Renshaw twisted the tip of the cane into the carpet. He watched his wrinkled hand open and close around the curve of his cane. "World changers?" he asked blearily. "Is that how you see yourself, Mr. Dysley, as the first in a generation of world shapers?" He shook his head.

"There is nothing new in what you seek from this trial," he said simply. "In fact, what you seek is as old as the first thoughts of mankind which went beyond the natural world of plants and animals that surrounded him. Why else would our ancestor-kings have mobilized entire civilizations with the solitary goal of crafting an eight-hundred-foot-high pyramid from over two million two-ton blocks of stone and covering thirteen square acres of land? Why else would they have constructed great temples which served no practical use, but were solely meant to establish a link between their king and the world beyond; a world where gods in chariots pulled the sun across the sky each day, requiring virgin sacrifices and beating hearts to be laid upon the altars of their temples in order to appease them to keep their schedules? What else besides the fear of the intangible, unknown spirit world could possess men to do such massive, irrational works?

"And from the looks of things these days with your trial, Mr. Dysley," Renshaw continued, sounding a little disappointed, "we haven't changed a bit over the last four thousand years.

"You and I, Mr. Dysley," he said, "are simply a part of man's most recent effort to find what seems to have eluded us all of these centuries."

Will was intrigued by Renshaw's words, though he would never admit it. He wasn't sure where the old man was taking him, but he was confident that he could hold his own wherever it was. He decided to play along.

"And what is it we've been seeking, Professor?"

Professor Renshaw again toyed with the tip of his cane in the carpet.

"Comfort," he said plainly.

"Comfort?"

"Yes, comfort," Renshaw repeated. "Every time a heart was cut out with a knife from the living body of a virgin and laid on a sacrificial altar, our ancestors were seeking assurance that the godly reinsman of the chariot would not fail to make his daily journey across the sky. They sought comfort that the strange, brilliant orange ball would rise over the horizon the next morning and give them light, and grow their crops, and warm their faces yet another day.

"Your temple is less tangible than those of our ancestors," Renshaw continued, "but your altar is certainly no less bloody. Your temple is the law, your knife is the tongue, and your altar is the courtroom."

Will began to pace the area in front of the windows. He had one hand deep in his pocket and the other rattled the stem of his pipe between his teeth.

"Let me ask you, Professor," he said inquisitively, "don't you find it odd that along the vast curve of history, we cannot point a finger at one single event which holds greater importance to the future of mankind than the story of the resurrection of Jesus Christ?

"Yet, for evidence of this unprecedented event, we have only the reports of a couple of angels or gardeners, depending on who is telling the story, an empty tomb, and the words of twelve men of questionable intellect and character. Where is the comfort in that, Mr. Renshaw? Where is the comfort in not knowing the truth? Or are we to derive comfort from ignorance when it comes to spiritual things?"

Will took a long draw on his pipe and released a rush of smoke which, the insightful wisdom of Professor Renshaw guessed, had seen his very soul.

"Where would we be in other areas of life," he continued, "if we had left things as we found them? Where would we be without the pioneers of knowledge?

"Men like Charles Darwin, who dove headlong into the then-mysterious world of the life sciences and opened up the natural world to the mind of man, upturning stones that many felt should have been left alone. As a result of Darwin's efforts, we have the system of evolution which we can point to for answers to the origin of life in our physical world.

"You are a scientist, Professor Renshaw. How can you sit back and allow an entire world to go unexplored, a world which surrounds us and influences us right down to the very date we write on our notepads!"

Will wandered back to his desk, where he tapped out the remains of the bowl of tobacco he'd been smoking. Professor Renshaw watched him intently.

"What we need, Professor," he said, setting down his pipe, "is a system which will provide us with answers in the spiritual world—a system like we have with Darwin's evolution in the world of nature."

Rubin Renshaw smiled and narrowed his eyes at the man before him.

"And I suppose," said Renshaw, tracing the soft brim of his fedora, "that this trial is about you being the first to pioneer a system for the spiritual world which is to be the equivalent of Darwin's evolution in the natural?"

Will did not answer the professor; he sat down in his chair behind his desk. He swiveled toward the windows, where he watched the artificial light of the city replace the natural light of day.

"I know you are a man of fact," Renshaw continued, "because that is the nature of your profession. And it seems obvious by the line of argument you have chosen for the defense that you do not believe in miracles, and there are many in the world who would agree with you.

"Yet, in the course of your fact-filled lives, you and many other people walk right over what I like to call 'the missing miracles' of our world, like diamonds in the mud. The first and I feel the most important of these missing miracles is best relayed with a story—if you have the time, sir. The story of a skull found in a gravel pit."

Dysley lay back in his chair. He folded his hands across his chest and stared out the window at the rich blues and blacks of the evening sky. His silence gave Renshaw the freedom to continue.

Professor Renshaw paused a moment, then began: "In 1911 in a fossil pit near Piltdown Common, England, an ancient human skull was reported to have been unearthed. The skull was thought to be a million years old.

"The curious thing about the skull and what separated it from the other ancient human skulls in archaeological museums around the world was that it had roughly the same size cavity for the brain as modern man. Yet this modern brain cavity was attached to a primitive ape-like face.

"You spoke earlier about Charles Darwin and the theory of evolution, Mr. Dysley," Renshaw continued. "Well, this find was the most powerful evidence to date in support of Darwin's hypothesis. The million-year-old skull which came to be called the Piltdown Skull supported the notion that the forces of natural selection had worked on the human brain just as it had every other organ on every other creature on Earth. Darwin's theory appeared to be watertight. It appeared to be as accurate in its explanation of the origin of man as it was in explaining the origins of plants and animals.

"The discovery of the Piltdown Skull enabled scientists to surmise that man's brain had evolved through natural selective forces over a million-or-more-year period of time, making the slow transition from cave dweller to city dweller, from rock thrower to missile launcher, from cave painter to space station architect. With the addition of the Piltdown Skull, evolution was sound theory for the origin of mankind.

"But something did not sit right with another scientist in the time of Darwin. His name was Alfred Russel Wallace, and although you have probably never heard of him, he is given credit by the scientific community as the co-discoverer of evolution. In his study of native peoples of the tropics, Wallace ran into a stumbling block for his and Darwin's theory.

"Wallace observed that the natives on these remote islands possessed a brain capable of far more than what was needed to survive. These native people, Wallace discovered, had a brain with essentially the same mental capacity as his own. And, he surmised, if natural selection was truly the force involved in shaping the brains of these natives, then they should have had brains only slightly more developed than those of apes. What use were the complex hidden reaches of the brain to the simple, food-gathering lifestyles of these people? Wallace asked.

"In studying the natives further, Wallace found that other organs which related to the brain had also developed far in excess of what the tenets of change under natural selection provided for. The voice box, for example, was capable of inflection and modulation on a par with any of the most eloquent speakers back in England. For what reason covered by the scope of the theory of evolution had this occurred?"

Professor Renshaw leaned forward on his cane.

"This question led to others which began to form in Wallace's mind," he continued. "What natural competitor of man had caused him to develop skills in mathematics and the creative arts? How does a prolonged and helpless human infancy fit into a harsh environment of predator and prey? Where along the evolutionary spectrum did natural forces dictate that man should abandon instinct? What had caused the human brain to evolve further than a particular environment required?

"Wallace brought these questions back with him to England and laid them before Darwin himself. But Darwin, having read Wallace's work, is reported to have scrawled, 'No, no, no,' in bold letters across the front page.

"Wallace felt that he had discovered the weak link in a theory which was, in essence, his own, and unearthed what I consider to be one of the *missing miracles* which have been curiously set aside by the mass proliferators of knowledge."

Will Dysley swiveled forward to face the professor.

"So what of this Piltdown Skull?" Will said. "Certainly a million years is enough time for the brain to have evolved by the natural selective forces?"

Renshaw smiled. "Yes," he said, "it would have been, but it wasn't."

"What?" said Will, straightening up.

"In 1953, the Piltdown Skull was discovered to be a fake," Renshaw revealed. "The skull was the creation of a very knowledgeable hoaxer who had fooled the scientific community for nearly fifty years. Unfortunately for Darwin and the proponents of the theory of evolution, another ancient human skull had yet to be discovered to take the place of Piltdown.

"And to this day, the next in line is a skull dated at about eight thousand years.[2] That skull shows a modern brain box attached to a primitive ape-like face. Thereby proving, according to the authentic fossil record, that the human brain literally exploded onto the scene in mere moments, by the standards of natural selection theory.

"According to natural selection, eight thousand years is not enough time to lose the webbing between the toes of a duck let alone change the mind of man from a creature groveling in the dirt to a creature reaching for the stars."

"Your conclusion, Professor," Will demanded.

Professor Renshaw smiled at Will's judge-like overseeing of his story.

"My conclusion, Mr. Dysley, is the same as Wallace's: that there was another reason for the sudden increase in the cranial capacity of the human being. Wallace concluded that there must be another reason why our brain seemed to be the one organ in the kingdom of nature which went against the tenets of natural selection. A unique reason which explained why we had developed skills in math and music and art, and why we remain helpless children for such an unnaturally extended infancy, and why we abandoned the instincts of animals long ago. A reason which finds its home in theology and not biology."

Will Dysley began to laugh.

Renshaw looked puzzlingly at him.

....

"Professor Renshaw!" Dysley cried. "You and Wallace have obviously not thought this all the way through, my friend! I'm afraid you are committing a blunder at the kindergarten level, Professor! You're substituting the *absence of evidence* for the *evidence of absence!*" he scoffed. Will stood and walked round to the front of his desk.

"Don't you see, Professor?" he jeered. "You, like every other street-corner minister, are basing your conclusions on the lack of evidence and the lack of proof! The existence of God cannot be proven by what's missing!" He let out a sardonic laugh.

Rubin Renshaw grinned.

"Perhaps another of my diamonds in the mud will help you to understand my point," he said. "Have you heard of the Anthropic Principle, Mr. Dysley?"

Will gestured for him to proceed as if he was wasting his time.

"The Anthropic Principle refers to our most current studies of our world and the universe, specifically, the parameters which allow life to exist on Earth.

"These parameters, such as the Earth's distance from the sun, the thickness of the Earth's crust, right down to the mass of a neutron, seem to all be ideally set to the benefit of the existence of life. The more we learn about these parameters, the more we are astonished at the effect delicate variations in them would have on life on this planet.

"They seem to be precisely tuned to the benefit of man and other life on Earth. The ozone layer, and the effect we can have on it, is probably the most widely known of these parameters."

....

Dysley plopped down on the edge of his desk. "We've studied the ozone layer, Professor," he said matter-of-factly. "We've come to understand it. We have evidence that we are inversely affecting its function to protect the Earth from the harmful rays of the sun."

"Yes," agreed Renshaw, "we understand it and its function, but we do not understand why it is there in the first place—why it sits above the Earth so perfectly protecting us from the harmful elements of the sun, so precisely perfect for man to live out his years."

Renshaw straightened the stack of books on his lap. He half-chuckled to himself.

"After centuries of accumulated knowledge," he said, "we find ourselves in the same shoes of our ancestors, don't we? Cutting the beating heart from some hapless victim and laying it on our modern-day altars. We find ourselves, even now, gazing up in awe at the brilliant orange ball making its way across the sky, wondering why it doesn't just burn us into oblivion—or staring suspiciously in the mirror, trying to catch a glimpse of the primitive, instinctual mind of the ape-like creature some would place at the foot of our family tree. Yet the questions sought upon the stone altars and in the hollow eye sockets of the Piltdown Skull have reemerged in your court of law, Mr. Dysley, seeking the same ancient answer."

Will snatched his pipe from the ashtray and prepared to fill it with tobacco again. "And that's exactly what the trial is about, Professor," he said mockingly. "Finding evidence so we do not have to draw unsound conclusions from a bunch of old bones!"

Will stood agitatedly, and began to pace the floor again.

"I simply refuse to accept that a being as sovereign as you have alluded to in your Anthropic Principle," he said angrily, "who allegedly engineered the delicate placement of the parameters of life and interrupted nature's proven selective process in the development of the human brain, could possibly be so *negligent* in leaving a more concrete path of evidence to the *one momentous event* which makes or breaks his case. He creates thirteen billion light years of space in six days and leaves us with nothing more than the rumors of angels as evidence for the resurrection of his Son?

"I don't buy it!" Will said emphatically. "I ask you, Professor, how could God have made such a mistake?"

"Well, Mr. Dysley," said Renshaw plainly. "I see it precisely the other way. I wonder how a God capable of such exactness could possibly leave out evidence without a reason."

Will leered at the professor.

"Oh come now, Professor Renshaw!" he sneered. "Are you suggesting that God is actually withholding evidence from us?"

"In a way, yes," Renshaw said. "As you know, the story of man is not yet complete, Mr. Dysley."

Will returned to his desk and sat down with the obvious intent of ending the conversation. "Well, Professor," he said derisively, "I don't have time to wait; I plan to finish it for him. We've got a big day tomorrow; I suggest you get some rest. I want you fresh when you hit the stand."

Professor Renshaw nodded and lifted his hat from the stack of books that lay across his lap. His eyes widened when he saw the book which was on top of the stack, a Book of infallible harmony. It had a well-worn cover splitting and cracking from age. There were only pieces of the two-word, gold-embossed title remaining at the top of the cover. However, Rubin Renshaw did not need to read the title of the book to know what it was. The mere touch of its soft spine and he knew. He needed only to smell the deteriorating leather to know that this was an old friend.

He used his mahogany cane to push himself to his feet and cradled the stack of books under his arm. He turned with renewed strength to face Will Dysley.

"Brick by brick," the old scholar began, snugging the olive fedora down on his head, "like the ancient architects of the pyramids, or bone by bone, like the archaeologist-hoaxer of Piltdown, you gather your evidence and your facts, building your case, Mr. Dysley.

"But perhaps the answer you seek will require less of a craftsman and more of a magician."

Seated at his desk, Will Dysley narrowed his eyes at the old professor. Behind him, the darkness of night engulfed all but the disordered squares of light from offices in the buildings beyond.

"The God whose logic you question," said Renshaw, staring directly into the darkness, "is the God of the universe, Mr. Dysley. And it is his son you have laid on your altar. If I were in your shoes, I would bend a heedful ear to the three-word proclamation of the angels in the tomb that morning, sir—a heedful ear."

Rubin Renshaw swayed as he turned and picked his way to the door of the office. He latched the cane around his forearm and pulled open the door.

"I do not plan on pulling punches tomorrow, Mr. Renshaw," said Dysley to his departing guest, his voice carrying a hint of warning.

"All that you hear may not be to your liking; the character of those men you hold sacred will be attacked. Please do not let your beliefs get in the way of truth, nor your emotions in the path of justice."

Renshaw paused to listen to Will's final words, then slowly clicked the door shut behind him.

15

The Gospel According to Saint Will

"PROFESSOR RENSHAW," Dysley began as he strolled up to the witness stand carrying a Bible in his hand, "how many accounts do we have of what transpired at the tomb the morning the body of Jesus was first discovered to be missing?"

"Like the four winds of the Earth," Renshaw responded, "there are four accountings. They are known as the Gospels of Matthew, Mark, Luke, and John."

The cameramen in the four corners of the room suddenly felt important and fine-tuned the focus on their machines.

"And these are all found within these pages, Professor?" Will continued, flapping the Bible.

Renshaw nodded.

Will walked to the other side of his expert witness.

"Now, Professor," he said, "I want to concentrate on a very specific time frame in each of the four Gospels, and I do so to prove a very important point; so bear with me." Will flipped open the Bible.

"Let's start with Matthew," he said, opening to a marked place towards the back of the Bible. "Chapter twenty-eight, verses one through six. Could you please read those verses aloud for us, Professor?"

Renshaw opened the worn Bible he had brought with him to the stand. He located the verses in the Gospel of Matthew.

He read: "Now after the Sabbath, as the first day of the week began to dawn, Mary Magdalene and the other Mary came to see the tomb. And behold, there was a great earthquake; for an angel of the Lord descended from heaven, and came and rolled back the stone from the door, and sat on it.

"His countenance was like lightning, and his clothing as white as snow. And the guards shook for fear of him, and became like dead men.

"But the angel answered and said to the women, 'Do not be afraid, for I know that you seek Jesus who was crucified. He is not here; for he is risen, as he said. Come, see the place where the Lord lay.'" Renshaw looked up at Will, indicating that he had finished.

"OK, Professor," Will said as he turned back a few pages. "Now to Mark's account of the same time frame in the story. Chapter sixteen, verses one through six, again please, Mr. Renshaw."

"Mark," Renshaw thought aloud as he leafed through the delicate pages of the text. "Chapter sixteen, verse one."

And he read: "Now when the Sabbath was past, Mary Magdalene, Mary the mother of James, and Salome bought spices, that they might come and anoint him. Very early in the morning, on the first day of the week, they came to the tomb when the sun had risen.

"And they said among themselves, 'Who will roll away the stone from the door of the tomb for us?' But when they looked up, they saw that the stone had been rolled away—for it was very large.

"And entering the tomb, they saw a young man clothed in a long white robe sitting on the right side; and they were alarmed. But he said to them, 'Do not be alarmed. You seek Jesus of Nazareth, who was crucified. He is risen! He is not here. See the place where they laid him,'" Renshaw finished.

"On to Luke, Professor Renshaw," said Will, opening up to another tabbed page, "beginning with verse one of chapter twenty-four."

Renshaw was ahead of him, knowing this beloved book the way he did.

"Now on the first day of the week, very early in the morning, they, and certain other women, came to the tomb bringing the spices which they had prepared. But they found the stone rolled away from the tomb.

"Then they went in and did not find the body of the Lord Jesus. And it happened, as they were greatly perplexed about this, that behold, two men stood by them in shining garments—"

"Good," Dysley said, interrupting Renshaw's reading. "One more account by John . . . chapter twenty, verse one, please."

"On the first day of the week Mary Magdalene came to the tomb early, while it was still dark, and saw that the stone had been taken away from the tomb.

"Then she ran and came to Simon Peter, and to the other disciple, whom Jesus loved, and said to them, 'They have taken away the Lord out of the tomb, and we do not know where they have laid him.' Peter therefore went out, and the other disciple, and were going to the tomb.

"So they both ran together, and the other disciple outran Peter and came to the tomb first. And he, stooping down and looking in, saw the linen cloths lying there."

"Good, Professor; thank you, sir," said Will. He then turned to the courtroom audience, "And thank you all for listening."

Will began to pace in a semicircle in front of the witness stand, facing the audience, his hands characteristically clasped behind his back.

"I think you may have already guessed why I've asked my witness to read these verses of Scripture," he said. "The verses are supposed to be describing the exact same space of time; but they are, as you just heard, very different accounts.

"In my preparation for this trial, I tried to give the disciples the benefit of the doubt. I knew there were bound to be some variations in their accounts of the events surrounding the resurrection, but I thought that the differences would be within reason.

"We know from my cross-examination yesterday that there appeared to be some intellectual inferiority among the disciples; they seemed to be unable to catch the drift of what Jesus was trying to tell them about his promise to rise from the grave. However, some people far removed from Christ were able to understand, including Pontius Pilate. So what's the reason for the discrepancies in the four accounts about the discovery of the missing body?

"What caused Matthew to write of an earthquake caused by an angel rolling away the stone at the tomb—an event that no other disciple recorded?

"Mark's empty-tomb visitors find the stone already rolled away. Luke writes of two men at the site of the empty tomb; Matthew and Mark write of a single person being there, and they say he was an angel.

"And, Professor," said Dysley, turning back to his witness, "were there any men or angels in John's description?"

"In the Gospel of John," Renshaw said with a searching voice, "it is Christ himself who confronts Mary when she returns to the tomb."

"Christ himself?" Will repeated. "Not an angel or a couple of men, but Jesus himself. Interesting."

Will tapped his chin pensively. "Now, how many women did Mark have at the tomb that first morning, and how many did John?"

"Three for Mark, and one for John—just Mary Magdalene," Renshaw answered.

"Just the hooker Mary?" Dysley asked with a sarcastic nod.

A few of the people in the courtroom found humor in the ridiculous exchange which had sort of blossomed into something like an Abbott and Costello *Who's on First* routine. The viewers at home laughed and felt like they were watching an episode of "Nightcourt."

"What's causing all of this confusion?" Will asked rhetorically, turning back to the courtroom crowd. "Is it the intellectual inferiority thing again, or some other weakness common to mankind, some other human short-fall which we do not have to look far to find, some other *miracle-destroyer* lurking deep in the imperfect mind of man? Let's look at a few other things and maybe the answer will hit us square in the face."

Dysley maneuvered to the side of his witness.

"Professor, would you agree that these women who came to the tomb were experiencing feelings of profound depression at the death of Jesus Christ?"

Renshaw nodded.

"They believed the Romans had unwittingly executed the Son of God," said Renshaw plainly. "That probably caused a fair degree of duress and depression, yes."

"And they had watched him die, didn't they, sir?"

"Yes, the women were present at the crucifixion."

"They saw him humiliated, spat on, whipped, beaten?" Will looked over at Clive's witness Dr. Jonas, who had been so graphic in his recounting of what had happened to Christ.

"Yes."

"They read the sign mocking all that Christ claimed to be," Will continued. "A sign that read sarcastically: 'The King of the Jews,' in Hebrew, Greek, and Latin, so no one would miss out on the joke?"

"Yes."

"What relation were these women to Christ?"

"Mary Magdalene was the prostitute whom Jesus forgave, and the other Mary was the mother of James and Joseph, the wife of Clopas."

"These were the women telling their stories to the authors of the four Gospels?"

"Yes."

Will took a stroll over to the jury box.

"So," he said bluntly, addressing the jury, "it's fair to say that there were some heavy human emotions involved in the accuracy of the accounts we just read. We have two women—who loved Jesus dearly—going to the tomb early in the morning while it was still dark, according to Saint John. At the tomb, they experienced a sequence of events that obviously, by the vast number of discrepancies we've noted, even they themselves were not quite sure of.

"For all we know," Will said, "it could have happened this way."

He walked back to his table and picked up his notepad.

"I present the Gospel according to Will."

The people in the audience and at home thought they should want to laugh at this, but they found that they couldn't. There was something about all this that wasn't funny anymore, something about this that was self-incriminating to them in general as a race, something that was getting very serious.

Will cleared his throat and read from his notes.

"The two grief-stricken Marys had seen Jesus, who preached that he was as powerful as God himself, nailed to a cross and buried in a tomb. Mary the wife of Clopas and Mary Magdalene," Will looked up from his notes, "the hooker, whose only friend had been Jesus, go to the area of the tombs early on the first day of the week after the Sabbath and encounter a man at the entrance to an open tomb.

"The man, who was probably a grave digger or a gardener, immediately assesses from the looks on the two women's faces that they are about to conclude incorrectly about what they're seeing. He says to them, 'Do not be afraid; I know that you seek Jesus of Nazareth, who was crucified.' To this the grave digger receives no response from the women—only puzzled, intense expressions of fear and wonderment."

Will mimicked the expression he depicted to be on the women's faces for the jury.

"So, he tries again. 'He is not here,' he says to them, 'see the place where they laid him.' And he points to a tomb two down along the row of tombs—a tomb which still has the large stone covering its entrance, and where Christ's lifeless, decaying body remains safely inside, very much dead.

"The two Marys, in a state of blind emotion and more than ready to believe anything except that the Romans were able to get away with crucifying their Savior without the wrath of God raining down on them, believe that the grave digger is pointing into the empty tomb which he is standing in front of—a grave that he is actually preparing for someone else. They run off hysterically to tell the disciples before the grave digger can explain any further.

"The disciples, also engulfed in the emotion of the moment and their love for Christ, are quick to record the stories of the women, thereby immortalizing a simple grave digger, elevating him—by Mark's account—to the rank of an *angel,* and altering the course of human history forever."

Will is on a roll, thought his partner Tom Weber back at the table.

This is getting good, admitted the media managers who were watching the drama back at the studios. *"L.A. Law" never had a script like this,* they thought in unison.

"The reverberations of their writings which, even now, careen off the walls of this courtroom two thousand years later," Will said, gazing around at the regal courtroom, "all because two women who were overrun with fear and depression—common human emotions—were ready to buy into anything except the truth as they went to the wrong tomb that fateful morning."

An acrid smirk spread across Will's face.

"A rather *grave error,* wouldn't you say?" he jeered to the judge.

He paused a minute, turning to the jury. He put his hands on the jury box railing.

"You and I both know," he said candidly, "this is not an unusual reaction for the grief-stricken. The mother of a man missing in action during wartime is quick to see her son in the photograph brought back from Cambodia, even though all the evidence points to the contrary. The photo could be a mannequin in a store window and yet she would still see her son; it's simply the common human reaction to severe feelings of loss. We're all painfully aware that at times of anguish we sometimes see what we want to see and hear what we want to hear regardless of the reality of the moment.

"And to think that we have so long accepted the events surrounding the resurrection as having their origins in mystery and miracle," Will chuckled a little sadly, "when if we would just take a look at ourselves and the failings of humanity, then the less-than-miraculous becomes the much more plausible explanation. The miracle-destroyers seem to reveal themselves every time we look at ourselves in the mirror."

Will slapped the soft cover of the Bible somewhat dejectedly against his palm; the soft puff echoed in the dead silence of the courtroom.

He returned to his table. His head was down and he remained standing.

The people in the courtroom seemed subdued with a heavy blanket of sadness and realization. The people at home watching the trial on television felt the same way; they almost felt like reaching for the remote.

"The everyday, common weaknesses of humanity," Will said, before they had a chance, filling their screens with a close-up of his dispirited eyes, "emerge as the truly believable explanation of the story which threatens to open a pathway for prayer and Christianity into our public schools, and not some divinely orchestrated miracle."

Will sank slowly into his chair.

"Your witness," he said.

16

Ace in the Hole

FRANKLY, the media people couldn't believe their luck.

Finally someone else was saying exactly what they had been saying all along.

Finally they knew they weren't alone in their far-and-wide search for examples of human weakness which they so passionately splashed across their newspapers and video monitors. At last the negativity of mankind could be their focus for weeks on end, and they didn't even have to look very hard. Will Dysley was laying it all out for them in front of their rolling cameras.

Better still, he was showing them that the theme which they stuck to so religiously in their publications and broadcasts was not at all a new pattern in the human story, but that it was indeed very, very old—at least as ancient as the characters in the story of the resurrection. He also illustrated that no one was immune to shortcomings, including the disciples of Jesus Christ himself, and that we are all, as the media monsters have cried for years, created equal for purposes of success or, sensationally, for purposes of failure.

As a self-commemoration of this self-proclaimed vindication, the newspaper magnates decided to devote entire issues to the reporting and commentary of the Jesus Trial. Their readers, getting their daily sour mouthful of empty-calorie literature, could've sworn they noticed a we've-been-right-all-along bent to the editorials, but no one thought to argue about it.

You see, there comes a point when people become so far removed from truth that they no longer recognize it when it stands before them. Little did they know the battle they were petitioning and lobbying against was being fought on painted streets and found its origin in a curious interplay of the real and the perceived, between electrical wires and the synaptic wiring of the human mind. Only the mechanism was real and it had long ago been infiltrated—and it was obvious by now, rotten to the core.

All the press pandemonium did not, however, halt the austere flow of due process. Everyone in the courtroom had returned to their seats after the recess for lunch and a slightly dejected Randell Clive was about to begin his cross-examination of Professor Rubin Renshaw.

Clive took a deep breath and tried to tell himself it wasn't over yet. He lifted his head with renewed conviction, pulling a good deal of strength from the pleasant, innocent smiling face of little Mary and the encouraging nod of her mother seated next to him.

He stood energetically and walked toward the aged scholar on the witness stand.

"Professor Renshaw," he said, "you seem well-versed in the history of Christianity."

"Yes sir, I am," said Renshaw humbly.

"I would assume that you know the name of the city in which Christianity originated?"

Renshaw nodded.

"Please share that with us, Professor," Clive motioned at the jury.

"Jerusalem," said the professor.

"Jerusalem?" asked Clive.

"Yes."

"The same city where Christ was crucified?" Clive said, baffled.

"The same, yes," said Renshaw.

"Interesting."

Clive rested his elbow on the witness stand. "Professor, who were the progenitors of Christianity?" he continued. "Who were the people trying to spread the word?"

"The disciples," said the professor.

Clive turned quickly to face Renshaw.

"You're telling us, sir, that the disciples went right back to the city—where the crucifixion occurred—to begin their ministries?" Clive vexed.

"No," said Renshaw modestly, "history tells us that, not me, sir."

"Then it is a historical fact that Christianity started in Jerusalem?"

"Yes, sir."

Clive nodded his head as if to say, "I see."

"And how soon after the death of Christ did the disciples begin their ministries?" he asked.

Renshaw studied the ceiling, trying to recall the correct figures. Clive tapped his foot, waiting for the response.

"I believe the disciples first preached Christianity within weeks after the crucifixion," he recalled.

"Within weeks," Clive repeated. "And from there the word spread, didn't it Mr. Renshaw, until Christianity had a massive following?"

"Yes, the word spread very quickly from there."

"And how did the Romans feel about this?"

"They were displeased."

"So what did they do to stop it?"

"Everything in their power, Counselor," Renshaw chuckled. "Christianity was a threat to the fundamentals of Roman life and to the theocratic beliefs of the Palestinian Jews. You must understand," he continued, "back then, religion was at the center of society."

"Yet Christianity continued to spread, didn't it, Professor?" Clive interjected. "Despite the efforts of the authorities to squelch the new movement, Christianity flourished among the people, and was soon being preached on street corners all around the Mediterranean.

"History tells us this too, Professor," he added irrefutably.

Clive paused for a moment, caressing the contours of his chin.

"And what was it they were saying on those street corners, Professor?" he asked. "What was the focus of the message?"

"The cornerstone of Christianity has always been the cross," Renshaw responded directly.

"The cross?" said Clive. "What about it?"

"Christ dying for the remission of our sins on the cross."

"Not only dying, Professor, but what?"

"Rising again."

"Exactly, Mr. Renshaw!" Clive cried, shocking the jury into heightened attention. "The resurrection!"

Renshaw nodded.

"Christ's resurrection from the tomb was at the core of the new religion!" Clive confirmed. "His resurrection from a tomb which lay just on the outskirts of the city of Jerusalem, the very same city where the disciples began their preaching of Christianity?" he asked, bewildered.

Elizabeth grabbed hold of her daughter's hand excitedly. *Maybe it had all been worth it,* she thought—the disruption of her and her daughter's lives, the mental pressure of being the one to bring such a controversial issue to trial, the constant media harassment.

Maybe, she dearly hoped for the precious life sitting next to her, *Randell Clive and this case could change things for the better in the public school systems and in the world. Maybe this trial would make people see things differently, the way that she saw them.*

Her attorney's motives were good, but not entirely all that pure.

He shot a wry smile at his archrival seated at the table for the defense.

And for a brief moment, the people at home found themselves filling with hope and they actually started rooting for the longshot—the underdog.

"Most certainly," Clive continued, "a synthesis of the four Gospel accounts reveals a complete picture of what actually took place that first Easter morning devoid of contradiction, inerrable and consistent as is all of Scripture and a far cry from the unsubstantiated delirium of the gospel according to Saint Will," he gazed levelly at Dysley, his tone bearing perhaps a hint of long-deserved requital, "but that is a more intensive, detailed issue. The matter at hand, however, is a bit more plain."

Clive savored his stare for a good moment. He thought he saw Dysley's lips tighten, a slight firming of his jaw line, perhaps an indication that his blow had hit home.

"Now," said Clive sharply, pulling his eyes from Dysley and back to the jury, "whether or not the disciples' flaring emotions caused them to go to the wrong tomb that morning, certainly the Roman authorities had a line on the right tomb. They knew that that dead body in the tomb was their only ace in the hole.

"And, whether or not the disciples were too stupid to comprehend Christ's attempts to tell them about his plan to rise on the third day, Pontius Pilate certainly understood," Clive said sarcastically.

"He understood so well," Clive yelled, pointing at Dysley's table, "counsel for the defense has told us, that he sent a Roman guard unit to the tomb. He was trying to prevent exactly what ended up happening, wasn't he? Pilate knew very well his only hope of stopping the spread of Christianity was to keep the body of Christ safe and sound behind that boulder.

"Pilate knew indeed," Clive emphasized, "that without a body, his ship was sunk."

The counselor walked back to the witness.

"What I would like to know," he continued, resuming his relaxed stance, "is how the Roman and Jewish authorities lost their ace in the hole? I mean, as my opponent has told us, they had their highly trained military guard at the entrance and the disciples had no knowledge of Christ's promise. So who could've taken the body? Where did it go?" Clive shrugged. "I don't know."

Behind Clive's back, Rubin Renshaw tightened his lips to prevent his inward smile from breaking through.

"Do you know, Professor Renshaw?"

Renshaw almost smiled.

"Any of you in the jury know?"

Clive waited only for a brief moment before he proceeded.

"One thing is for sure: the Romans didn't have the body, or they would have pulled it out of the tomb and showed it to the people."

Clive turned to Renshaw.

"Professor," he said, "you mentioned earlier that the Romans and the Jews would have done everything in their power to stop the spread of the disciples' teachings because it threatened the fundamental structure of their societies. So, if they had the body, why didn't it occur to them to use it to stop all the nonsense?

"Surely one look at the limp corpse of their Savior," Clive gestured, "and they would all go home with their tails between their legs and forget about their new religion.

"But that's not what happened, is it, Professor?"

The aged scholar shook his head sternly, masking his delight at Clive's penetrating questions.

"History tells us a different story," Clive said bluntly.

"According to history—yes, according to the undisputed historical record—" Clive proclaimed, "what actually happened was that in the very city where Christ was crucified, one of the world's greatest religions got its illustrious start. This happened among people who had actually witnessed the crucifixion, and many of them wanted nothing more than for Christianity to disappear off the face of the Earth forever. Yet if you look on virtually any street corner in America, you'll see that it's still alive and kicking.

"Amazing, isn't it?" he said, scratching his cheek.

"And all the Romans or the Jews had to do to stop it was stroll down to a tomb not more than a stone's throw away from the street corner ministries of the disciples— a tomb where they claimed lay the crucified, lifeless body of Jesus Christ. Seems sort of elementary to me," he said plainly.

"So much so," he added, leering over at the table for the defense, "that perhaps even the emotionally distraught, intellectually inferior minds of the disciples might have been able to handle it."

He pivoted to return to his table. "Or, maybe it just wasn't all that easy," he said over his shoulder.

"No more questions, your Honor."

With that, Judge Alexander lifted himself from his prefabricated, mold-like position at the top of the tall podium. He folded his bifocals and slipped them into his pocket.

"This court will reconvene tomorrow morning," he warbled, making no effort to clear the phlegm from his throat.

He brought his mallet down with a bang.

"I think we've all had enough for now," he said wearily, and headed for his chambers.

17

Under the Knife

THE DRIVE THAT NIGHT to visit Samantha Hollimon at The Angel of Mercy Hospital was filled with analysis and assessment of the trial. Will reflected on the sequence of arguments which had transpired in the courtroom the past few days. He concluded that he couldn't have hoped for a better turn of events than if he had written the script himself. His years of experience had given him the perfect angle to combat the spiritually appealing argument of his old classmate.

He smiled confidently as he contemplated the specific wording he would use to dispel the points Clive had brought before the court in the cross-examination of his expert witness Professor Renshaw. His defensive posturing offered infinite angles on any truths Clive might argue by simply pitting what was commonly known about mankind against that which went beyond the limits of human knowledge and understanding. However self-incriminating and humbling those knowns were, Dysley knew, they were far easier to accept than the ambiguity of the faith-based unknowns Clive was presenting.

The defense was allowed one more shot at Renshaw, who had proven to be quite an ally despite the combative words exchanged the night before in Will's office. They were men from two different worlds, Will thought. Renshaw was a man from the world of myth and legend and faith, and Will was a man of evidence and fact from the world of reality. He wondered briefly if men from such divergent realms could ever find reconciliation and agreement. Regardless of their differences, the professor was cooperating rather nicely on the stand, his knowledge and credibility in turn lending validity and authenticity to Will's defensive arguments.

As he drove, Will could see the cars on the other side of the road being buffeted by the strong gusts of wind; the drivers were constantly swerving and correcting with their steering wheels to hold their path. *This had been an unusual winter,* he thought. The wind had not been this consistent and this disruptive of order for as long as most could remember, and people were beginning to wonder if it was ever going to stop. In fact, the wind's belligerent wrath seemed to be worsening as the days of the trial wore on, its intensity rising in step with the heightened drama in the courtroom. However, Will was traveling with the wind and was left unaffected by its hollow fury.

As he neared the entrance of the hospital, Will's thoughts turned to the predicament of his girlfriend Samantha Hollimon. The doctors still had no idea why she had lost feeling in her lower body. Both the spinal and cerebral MRIs hadn't revealed a clue as to what was blocking the neurological links between her legs and her brain. The next step would be to perform a spinal tap, which was an incredibly precise procedure. The danger of the spinal tap was that partial or complete paralysis could occur if the doctors were off by a mere fraction in their insertion of the rod into the spinal column.

It was up to the patient to give the doctors the green light to proceed with the delicate operation. And despite the demands of the trial, Will thought as he parked his car in the underground lot and rode the elevator to the fifth floor, he was glad he had made the choice to be there for Sam to help her make the decision.

"Oh, my," said Samantha Hollimon in a distant voice as Will rounded the corner of the doorway into her room, "look what the cat dragged in."

Sam was slumped in her bed mindlessly clicking the remote control. Will had halfway predicted he might encounter this type of cold reception from her. She was under a tremendous amount of stress. And to someone having to make a decision such as the one now facing her, everyone else's life always appeared easy and trouble-free. Through dealing with distraught clients as he did most of his life, Will knew that bitterness and anger were commonly expressed during this type of physical and emotional upheaval. He also knew that he had not devoted to his bedridden companion the amount of time expected of a seven-year relationship.

He approached her bed carefully and gave her a peck on the cheek. She was unresponsive.

"Hello, honey," he said atoningly.

"How is everybody's favorite story-destroyer," she scoffed bitterly, flipping over so that her backside faced him.

This was starting to be a regular maneuver for her, thought Will. He looked at her empathetically.

"What's that supposed to mean, Sam?" he asked.

"Well," she said facing the wall, "hasn't your conscience gotten to you yet?"

"Sam..." said Will, trying to calm her.

"How can you live with yourself?" she continued, rolling over to look at Will with bloodshot eyes that had obviously shed many tears. "I've read the headlines. You have all but won the case, Mr.... Mr.... Ralph Nader of the Bible!"

"Come on, honey, please," said Will with a slight chuckle. "This is all stemming from your frame of mind."

"What I don't see," said Sam, ignoring Will's analysis, "is how the government, by trying to keep religion out of public life, is actually affecting people's decisions about it so profoundly."

"You're not making sense, honey," said Will, setting aside his overcoat and sitting down on the bed.

Sam rolled her eyes upward. "The heck I'm not!" she screamed. "*If*—or I should say *when*—you win, people will no longer lend as much credibility to the story of Christ and the resurrection because our omnipotent government found the story had some supposed inconsistencies. And you are the one pointing them out for us!"

Sam tried to pull the bed sheet up over her, but Will's weight prevented her from doing so. She let the corner of the bed sheet drop and began to cry.

Will put his arms around her and gently stroked her hair.

"I mean, what's next for you?" Sam sobbed heavily. "You've taken on God and won. What's next?"

Will said nothing. He only stared blankly at the TV, which was droning indifferently in the corner of the room.

He pulled back from her and looked into her eyes. She broke into a teary smile.

"I'm sorry," she sobbed. "I—"

"I know," said Will comfortingly.

They embraced again.

"Anything new from the experts?" Will ventured, testing the waters to see if Sam was ready to talk about what was really on her mind.

Will felt Sam's head shake from side to side.

"Have you decided?" Will asked.

Sam nodded slowly.

"Yes," she said, her voice quaking.

Will did not need to ask what she had decided.

"I think it's best to know, too," he said evenly. "Better to know now while something can still be done."

Sam blinked slowly and nodded again.

"When can they schedule you?" he asked.

Sam shrugged. "Tomorrow afternoon," she said softly, lifting her downcast eyes until they met Will's.

"Everything's going to be all right," he said consolingly.

Sam's expression suddenly brightened.

"How's Tyler?" she asked, smiling lovingly.

"Fine," said Will. "Except for his late-night visits to my study, he's been a perfect houseguest."

"Is he asking a lot of questions?" Sam winced. "I'm sorry if he is disturbing your work for the trial. Sometimes it's tough to get the kid to bed on time, even for his mother."

"He's fine," said Will. "Overly curious, but fine."

Will stood up and grabbed his overcoat.

Sam looked up longingly at him.

"You're going to be fine, Sam," he said reassuringly. "I'm sorry I can't stay longer."

"I understand," said Sam with one last sniffle.

"I'll check in with you after the procedure," he said and kissed her again. "I have to be in court early tomorrow. You may think it's over, but I still have to convince the jury," he smiled. "I'll call you from the office tomorrow evening."

Sam wiped away the last of her tears and smiled broadly.

"Hey, Mr. Nader," she laughed. "Are you sure you don't have something you want to ask me before I go under the knife?" Sam wiggled the empty ring finger on her left hand.

Will stopped in the doorway. "I promise after the trial we'll spend more time together," he said.

"That's not what I meant," she said mischievously.

Will returned her playful smile. He said nothing and stepped out into the hallway, his mind already on the next morning's work at the courthouse.

18

The Miracle-Destroyer

"COUNSEL FOR THE DEFENSE will begin the final redirect of his witness," said Judge Alexander, causing all present to cease their shuffling about.

Counselor Dysley set aside the pipe he had been fiddling with and arose from the table. He glared over at Randell Clive and pulled his perfectly pressed navy blue suit tightly by the lapels. He straightened his conservative but not altogether boring tie so that it lay straight down the front of him.

"Well," he said, loud enough for all to hear, "let's see if we can't show Counselor Clive what happened to Pontius Pilate's ace in the hole."

He walked out slowly toward the jury.

"In each of my arguments thus far," he said commandingly, "I've used words taken right from the horse's mouth, so to speak—words taken directly from the Bible in order to prove my point. This round will be no different.

"Let's concentrate," he said, veering off toward the witness stand, "on one of the characters in our story, Professor Renshaw. And specifically, on a character I believe was instrumental to the making of the myth of the resurrection of Christ.

"Do you still have your Bible handy, Mr. Renshaw?"

Renshaw lifted his old Bible from his lap.

"Look for the Gospel of John, chapter nineteen, verse thirty-eight, if you would please."

Renshaw thumbed through the text and located the verses.

"Read them for us, Professor."

The old scholar nodded and cleared his throat.

"After this, Joseph of Arimathea," he read, "being a disciple of Jesus, but secretly, for fear of the Jews, asked Pilate that he might take away the body of Jesus; and Pilate gave him permission. So he came and took the body of Jesus."

"OK," said Will. "Thank you, sir, and I'll try to get you off the stand as soon as I can. You've been up here a long time; I realize that.

"Professor," he continued, "what else can you tell us about this Joseph of Arimathea?"

Renshaw glanced at the ceiling, searching his memory.

"History records that he was a wealthy man and a member of the Sanhedrin, which was a group of Jewish men who counseled the Romans on the complexities of Jewish law and society."

"Were there a great number of differences in the laws and customs of the Jews and Romans, Professor?"

"Oh, yes, countless differences."

"There is one clear difference which directly relates to the reason Christ was ultimately sentenced to be crucified," said Will. "Can you describe it for us, Professor?"

"Well," said Renshaw, "most people do not know that it was actually the Jewish religious leaders who first sought to have Christ permanently removed from the scene. And it was before a non-Roman tribunal which Christ first stood trial."

"The Jewish leaders?" Dysley queried, trying to reinforce the difference in the minds of the jurists. "Not the Romans?"

"Yes," confirmed the professor, "the Jewish scribes, Pharisees, and Sadducees. They first brought Jesus before a Jewish court under charges of blasphemy since Christ repeatedly referred to himself as "the Son of God"—he was called the King of the Jews—and they found him guilty as charged. Yet, under Jewish law, the crime of blasphemy did not warrant the penalty of death by crucifixion, which is exactly what the Jewish religious leaders had in mind for Christ.

"Under Roman law, however, anyone claiming to be a king was a direct affront to the monocratic rule of Caesar. Therefore, Christ's claim that he was a king was an offense punishable by death.

"So," Renshaw continued, "the clever Jewish leaders brought Christ to Pilate under charges that he had proclaimed himself a king. They hoped that the Romans would convict him and sentence him to be nailed up on a cross of wood."

"Politics was alive and well even back then, eh, Mr. Renshaw?"

"Yes, sir, very much so."

"Now, sir, back to this man Joseph of Arimathea," said Will. "Professor, is it safe to assume that as prominent a man as he was in Jewish society—a man of wealth and political connections and a member of the Sanhedrin—would have been involved in some of the deliberations concerning Jesus while he was still alive; namely, what was to be done with him?"

"Yes, sir," said Renshaw, "since Christ's influence on the people plagued both the Jewish and the Roman leadership, it is likely that the members of the Sanhedrin were included in the discussions."

"They were the official go-between," Will reiterated, "as you mentioned, the experts between the two vastly different cultures?"

Renshaw nodded.

"May I have your Bible, Professor?"

Renshaw handed Will the book.

"Your Honor," said Will, waving the Bible in the air, "if it please the court, I would like to read the passage that the Professor read earlier, because there is a very important phrase which may shed some light on the reason the Roman authorities could not simply walk to the tomb on the outskirts of the city, as counselor Clive argued, and produce the body of Christ in order to squelch the spread of Christianity."

Judge Alexander motioned for him to proceed.

"And remember," Will said, again flapping the Bible in the air, reminding the jury of the source of the words he was about to read. He flipped his reading glasses onto the bridge of his nose.

"After this, Joseph of Arimathea," he read, "being a disciple of Jesus, but secretly, for fear of the Jews," he stopped reading. "Let's go at that one more time," he said, walking over to the jury box. "Joseph of Arimathea, being *a disciple of Jesus, but secretly, for fear of the Jews*"?

Will looked bewilderedly over his glasses at the jurists. "Then the passage goes on to say," he continued with disbelief in his voice, that Joseph "asked Pilate that he might take away the body of Jesus; and Pilate gave him permission. So he came and took the body of Jesus"!

Dysley grinned wickedly.

"A couple things bother me here," he said plainly.

"First, we have a man who held a prominent position in both camps of the enemies of Christianity or, at the least, he had ties with them. Second, we have a man who, the Bible tells us, is actually a disciple of Jesus, and who has managed to keep his religious affiliations a secret from his fellow members of the Sanhedrin council.

"Third, Joseph of Arimathea was most likely present at the discussions in which the Romans revealed their knowledge of Christ's promise to rise from the tomb. This knowledge, we've already established, somehow eluded the dull minds of the disciples despite Christ's numerous attempts to make them understand.

"And fourth, it says right here...," Will exclaimed, tapping hard on the cover of the Bible, "...that Pilate actually entrusted the dead body of Christ to the care of this man!"

Will abruptly removed his glasses. He looked directly at the eyes of the jurists.

"Do you see what's happening here?" he asked them.

"I think we've discovered the first documented case of political corruption!" he exclaimed. "Definitely the first ever among the followers of Christ!"

Will padded around the courtroom, letting his words be absorbed.

"I submit," he continued forcefully, "that Joseph of Arimathea bit his tongue in the meetings where his colleagues plotted the death of Christ, and concocted a superior scheme: a scheme which would give far more propulsion to the Christian movement than any feeble petition he might make to spare the life of Jesus.

"I submit that the body of Christ, in the hands of this clever politician, ended up *anywhere* other than where it was supposed to be," Will said with conviction. "Perhaps he dumped it in a collective grave filled with the bones of a hundred slaves, or he carried it off into the desert under the darkness of night, and buried it in a shallow grave in some secret place."

Randell Clive put his head down. His lifelong dreams were fading as quickly as Will's were emerging. He had matched wits with the best, and apparently, he had lost. He looked over at Elizabeth, who gave him a comforting smile.

Little Mary Magellan was absent from the trial today. Elizabeth had requested that she be allowed to miss the remaining days of the trial. It was senseless, Judge Alexander agreed, for the little girl to be exposed to the sometimes disturbing complexities of the trial.

Elizabeth had entrusted her precious daughter to the care of her sister, who had picked up Mary that morning for the drive to the north side of the city where she lived. Mary would be better off there with her, Elizabeth told herself—anywhere but here in this courtroom, where Christ and his disciples were being used like dixie cups and being dragged through the mud by the counsel for the defense.

"It's no wonder," Dysley continued, "Pilate's ace in the hole, as Mr. Clive called it, came up missing. You and I know enough about politicians and the lengths they'll go to attain their political aspirations."

Will walked back to his table and sat hunched on the edge.

"And what was at stake here?" he asked rhetorically. "Judging from the passage we read earlier, in Joseph's estimation there was more at stake than his name on the door of a high political office, as is the motivation for corruption for most modern-day politicians. No, there was much more at stake than any mortal man could hope to attain.

"What Joseph sought was immortality," Will said simply. "A guaranteed ticket to the kingdom of heaven. Well, Joseph should have realized that there are no guarantees in this life. It may have taken us two thousand years to expose his underlying political motivations, but we've done it.

"And the truth is, we are not surprised—not in the least bit. The character of the men and women surrounding this event are flawed and riddled with evidence of ulterior motives—motives we would have struggled with had we been in their shoes.

"All this means is that we can safely add another notch to our sad confession of the realities of human potential. Our list continues to grow, a list which is all too familiar to us.

"We can now add political corruption to our list of human weaknesses. We've uncovered the disciples' intellectual inferiority and subsequent loss of credibility as the authors of the Gospels, and we've revealed the emotional irrationality of the women at the tomb which lead them to believe what they wanted to believe, regardless of the reality of the situation.

"We can conclude with certainty," Will continued, "that these weaknesses offer us a far more plausible explanation to the truth of what occurred between the crucifixion fields and the charnel houses of ancient Jerusalem—more plausible than the miracle Mr. Clive would have us believe.

"Instead of accepting a miracle which goes against the grain of all we know to be possible, we are forced by these ancient examples of human frailty and error to remember and accept everything we know to be true about ourselves.

"Perhaps that is the reason this myth of the resurrection was created in the first place," said Counselor Will Dysley, his eyes downcast and introspective, "so that we would not have to look at our reflections in the mirror and see ourselves for what we truly are."

Will Dysley remained staring downward, lost in thought for a long moment.

When he looked up, he saw the eyes of the entire human race upon him.

He had not realized it, but the people in the court-room had grown still and silent while he spoke, as had the millions of viewers at home, all seemingly paralyzed by his incriminating words. And now they just stared hopelessly at him.

And Will felt a sudden weight bearing on his shoulders. His frame appeared to sag as he turned to head toward his table. The cameraman in the back corner zoomed in close on him so that the millions of viewers around the globe saw the transformation in his eyes. They saw the faintly glowing embers in his pupils flicker, then die, leaving only coal black. They saw him trudge sloth-like across the courtroom floor, burdened with the disappointment of a million disobedient children. They saw him pick his way carefully around the fiery fissures and the twisting, descending crevices in the fragile crust of human morality.

"That is all I have, your Honor," he said morosely, and sat down.

Judge Alexander rose from his position of presidency over the historic trial.

"This court will reconvene the day after tomorrow to hear the Counselors' closing comments," he said sternly.

He brought his gavel down solidly, closing the day's proceedings.

19

Impending Victory

TOM WEBER WAS grinning ear to ear as he and Will entered their prestigious law firm, his doubts turned to cheers. In one hand he carried an old bottle of brandy that he had been saving for a special occasion, in the other, two sparkling, full-bellied crystal glasses.

The congratulatory words from the members of the *Legal Entourage* were left outside the heavy oak doors of Will's office as the two partners prepared to celebrate in private the impending victory in the trial.

Tom's plump cheeks flushed with red as he twisted the corkscrew into the cork top of the dusty bottle. Will took a seat behind his desk and pulled his pipe from his breast pocket.

"You were on fire this morning, my dear partner," Tom said admiringly, shaking his head with disbelief at

Will's flawless performance. "Since the day this case came along, I'd noticed a certain passion in you, unlike what I had seen in any case before."

Tom carefully worked the cork to the lip of the bottle until it opened with a gentle pop.

"I knew this one was special to you, Will," Tom continued, quickly glancing up at his partner to see the first puff of smoke rise to the ceiling. He poured the chestnut-colored liquid about two fingers deep into the belly of the crystal glasses and carried one over to Will, who thanked him with a nod. "Are you ever going to tell me why this case obsessed you so?"

Will blew a mouthful of gray smoke into the brandy glass and watched as it swirled up in slow, concentric currents along the transparent, rounded walls and spilled miasmically over the edge.

"It is just a trial like any other," said Will evenly, still staring down at the glass and the dissipating smoke. "Same cast of characters, same motives, same weaknesses," he said, then threw back a swig of the brandy.

Tom looked up at his longtime partner with surprise.

"You almost seem distraught over this stuff, Will," he said. "I thought you'd be gloating to me about your intuitive decision to put this case under our roof. This court decision is going to greatly affect the state and federal laws regarding public displays of religion. Our names will be on those changes," Tom said, pouring himself a second two fingers' full.

"We've changed the world," he declared, raising his glass dramatically in triumph, "just like we've always dreamed of doing."

Will raised an eyebrow at his partner and stuck his pipe back between his teeth. A faint buzz from the inter-office communication system interrupted his response.

"What is it, Gladys?" he asked, holding down a button on his phone.

"You have a call," said the high-pitched voice of the office manager.

"Put it through," said Will as he picked up the receiver.

Tom looked down and swirled his remaining brandy in his glass and watched as the heavy liquid tumbled and mixed against the backdrop of the lamplight, changing colors with flashes of golden yellow and eddies of acorn and oxblood brown.

"Uh-huh," he heard Will say.

He tossed the brandy into his mouth and it hit the back of his throat with an explosion of refined taste.

"Well how...?" he heard Will ask.

He reached for the dusty bottle and read the label again, marveling at the age and splendor of the brandy.

"When did it happen?" he heard Will inquire.

He glanced up at his partner and saw that he had a distressed expression on his face. He looked hard at Will, trying to read the nature of the phone call in the movements of his eyes.

"OK," he saw Will say.

"I'll see you there tomorrow," Will finished and hung up the phone.

Tom Weber's eyes begged his partner for an explanation as to why he looked so sickened by what he had just heard. But Will simply lowered his head and looked despairingly at him, then finished the last of his brandy.

20

Adoption

A CHILD, IT IS SAID, is like an empty glass. She is filled from the faucet of the people to whom she is most exposed in the formative years. It is their wisdom and understanding and knowledge which raises the level of the liquid in the glass and determines whether it will be pure or tainted and muddied from the world. If you look, and not necessarily so closely, you can see the spirit of the parent in the heart of the child.

Little Mary Magellan sat almost soundlessly in the backseat of her aunt's Mercedes, the white hood of her parka rimmed with white fur was still up over her curly blond hair. The inside of the car was chilled from the cold wind, which seemed to permeate the glass of the windows and to suffuse the metal of the exterior and leather of the interior.

Mary had to tilt her head back awkwardly in order to see clearly through the white tunnel inside the hood, naively unaware of the reason for her difficulties and the ease by which it could be remedied.

What she was struggling to see was a doll which she had propped up in her lap. Reddish-orange tousled hair spilled from the head of the doll, covering one of its vacant-blue kaleidoscope eyes. This was Mary's favorite doll, although Elizabeth sometimes wondered why. It was not the prettiest of dolls, nor the warmest, but it went everywhere with Mary. The doll had been around since Mary's birth, as had a bunch of others, but Mary chose this one to be her constant companion. She called it "Light"—Elizabeth supposed it was because of its light-catching eyes.

Children are to be seen and not heard. Whenever Mary was outside of her mother's care, these words of instruction rang in her ears. Had she been a little older Mary might have thought to ask what exactly those words meant, but as innocent as she was, that thought never even entered her mind. These were words spoken by her mother, and therefore, were not to be questioned. Perhaps in some act of instinctual fidelity, the little girl was aware of the difficulty of her mother's predicament: raising a child on her own. Mary listened to her mother, she was a good girl in every way, and not by accident. Careful, soft-spoken words from Elizabeth helped keep her young mind unspotted from the world, and especially from the innate impurity of the world-changing trial which she had indirectly caused and which now raged in a downtown courtroom miles to the south.

Mary caught the tail end of an over-the-shoulder smile from her Aunt Katelin, who checked on her every few miles on the way to her north-side apartment where she would be watching Mary for the duration of the trial. Mary smiled up at her, a smile that was seen only by the backward reflection of a single eye in the corner of the rearview mirror. Color flushed into Mary's soft, angelic cheeks so that they looked almost like the airbrushed colors on the puffy cheeks of the doll. She nearly giggled to see that her aunt was keeping an eye on her in such a fashion, but was able to stifle the noise, remembering her mother's words of instruction concerning the place of children. However, she could not contain the dazzling smile which seemed to neither begin or end with her mouth. Mary's entire face was part of her smiles, from her eyebrows to her chin to her ears—all seemed attached to her contagious bursts of expression.

Mary's aunt had been a big part of her childhood. Aunt Katelin was always ready to help her older sister when she was in a jam. Katie Magellan loved Mary as if she were her own little girl, and enjoyed their visits very much—as did Mary, because Aunt Katie would always take her to one of her favorite places on their visits.

Katelin lived more than comfortably on what is called Chicago's Gold Coast, in the Marina Towers to be exact. She was two years younger than Elizabeth, but had already established a firm, high-heeled toehold on a middle rung of the corporate ladder working for John Hancock Insurance in the company's huge monolith-like skyscraper off North Michigan Avenue. Katelin had hair the color of corn and wheat, with a bit of hay mixed in, in sharp disconformity to the downtown-girl image she was perhaps subconciously trying to portray. She wore her hair neat and straight, a state to which the wind seemed to vehemently object, taking every opportunity to toss and popple her hair until her suburbanite roots were clearly exposed. She also wore a vaingloriously appropriate long black wool coat with knee-high, low-heeled boots as well as a black derby hat with a pink flower centered on the brim. Katelin was young and still finding her way; she was allowed a bit of pretense and fiction before the dark days come.

As they rounded a wide bend in the interstate, Katelin caught a glimpse of the elegant, cosmopolitan building she called home through a narrow slit between the high rises. Each time Mary visited Katelin made it a point to take her niece to the garden-like setting on the rooftop of the building for a wondrous view of the city and the coastline of Lake Michigan. Standing on her tippy-toes and peering down on the Hot Wheel-sized cars and tiny people moving about on the streets below was one of Mary's favorite things to do. It seemed no matter how hot and muggy the weather was or how cold and blustery, Mary never wanted to descend from the rooftop to street level again.

The two Marina Towers were blanketed by what appeared to be a thin sheet of darkly tinted glass which followed the high contours of the twin cylinders then sagged gently into a shallow trough between them on both sides of the structure. Thus, from the street, they looked like a big, shiny pair of binoculars standing upright. To the people on board the back-up of airborne planes heading for O'Hare, the towers looked like the infinity symbol in mathematics, but to Mary they were the place where "we go way up into the clouds!" as she loved to scream while throwing her arms above her head.

"Uh, Aunt Katie," came a small voice from the backseat. "Are we there yet?"

Katelin Magellan smiled broadly. *What kid doesn't ask that question?* she thought, triggering her mind to loose, sunspotted images of she and her older sister nagging their parents nonstop through four states on family journeys when they were young.

"Almost," she said in a somewhat mock-excited tone as we tend to do with children, but she flashed a genuine, wide-eyed smile at Mary in the rearview mirror to overcome it.

Katelin also vaguely felt the odd sensation of evening the score for all those times she had asked that very question. This time, however, she was in the driver's seat instead of the backseat, and she had to admit, it felt kind of good. *How long can those strange little childhood feelings linger?* she thought to herself with a soft chuckle.

Aunt Katie signaled left and checked the blind spot over her shoulder. The traffic was heavy and the wind was fierce on this morning commute from the courthouse in the downtown area. Katelin figured that an extremely rushed morning and the unnerving tension of the trial were the reasons that Elizabeth had been so reluctant to break from the embrace with her daughter on the courthouse steps. Katelin then forced her eyes wide open, trying to shake these distracting small-talk thoughts from her mind and concentrate on the driving.

"We're almost there, Mary," she said assuringly. A powerful gust of wind buffeted the car despite the decades of German engineering that had gone into streamlining the aerodynamic design. Katelin's leather driving gloves crinkled tight over the wheel.

Mary answered only with a wide grin through her hooded parka, then her attention went back to Light, seated on her lap. She had brought along Light's outfit box, which lay on the seat next to her. She unhooked the two clasps and flipped open the lid. She chose Light's frilly dress from the box, a dress just like the one Mary had hanging in her closet at home.

Mary carefully unbuttoned Light's jumpsuit one snap at a time, getting ready to maneuver the doll's limbs from the clothes. By accident, as she removed the jumpsuit, Mary dropped Light on the floor. The vibrating engine under her, Light rolled exanimately on her back, her wide eyes staring blankly at the dome light on the ceiling.

Mary looked down at her fallen doll, then plaintively up at the rearview mirror.

"Oh, sweetie," said Katelin, hearing the soft thud of the doll on the carpet and peering back at Mary. "You've dropped Light," she said with a girlish frown, then returned her attention to the road. "Don't take your belt off, honey; we're almost home."

Mary felt the onslaught of tears, but again remembered her mother's words and held them back. She tried to satisfy herself with the box full of Light's clothes that sat beside her on the seat.

Mary's somewhat dejected play was interrupted by the gentle slowing force of the antilock brakes of the

Mercedes. Mary looked up to see them approaching a line of yellow booths and baskets that she had seen many times while driving with her mother. She knew that she would soon feel the teeth-chattering jar of tires going over swaths of grated road and hear the clinking of change from a purse. The window would then be rolled down and some shiny silver coins would be given to the blue-shirted person in the booth or dropped into the big white basket with the red neon arrow to make the white and orange striped slat of wood go up.

It was all quite confusing to her young mind, mainly because she could see no difference between this road and any of the other roads she had ever been on. Stretching her neck against the upper-body restraint of the seat belt, she saw the same not-so-smooth black pavement and the same dotted white lines and the same types of different-colored cars. She just couldn't imagine why the other streets were free and this one cost a couple of little silver coins every few miles. Looking over at the slightly miffed expressions on the faces of the drivers next to her, even little Mary could see that this was not a conclusion drawn solely from the logic-untried regions of the mind of a small child.

No matter how much forethought she put into her day, Katelin Magellan never seemed to have exact change for the toll booths on the interstates and highways surrounding the city. She dug deeply into her oversized purse for the brown leather coin purse that always seemed to escape her grasp.

As they pulled to a stop at one of the manned booths, she gave up on the coin purse and switched to her wallet.

The wallet was easy to find, but was hard to unzip with her driving gloves on. She used her teeth to grip the fingers of one glove and pulled it off her hand. She looked up like a warm puppy with a glove in her mouth trying to smile at the person who manned the booth, who was actually a woman of massive proportions who simply held out a chubby hand but looked off in the distance at departing traffic. The fat woman's eyelids seemed apathetically locked at half-mast and she wore a surgical mask over her nose and mouth with a slit cut in the area over the mouth, where dangled a smoldering cigarette.

Sort of counterproductive, thought Katelin as she nervously fished for a dollar bill in the side compartment of her wallet, hoping to fill the attendant's hand before one of the buttons on that hopelessly taxed government-issue shirt put her eye out or the guy behind her, who she could see through the rearview mirror, lost his patience.

BEEP! BEEP! Aggravated palms leaned hard on the horn while tightly held lips mouthed words better left unheard.

Mary was ignorant of all the tension building in the people around her. All she could tell was that Aunt Katie was preoccupied, and that this was an ideal opportunity to do what she had wanted to do for the last few miles.

Mary unbuckled her seat belt so she could reach Light on the floor.

Katelin received her change thanklessly from the attendant and accelerated along with about eight other cars from eight other booths whose drivers acted like they had just been given the green flag at Indy, and who would soon be competing for three lanes a couple hundred yards ahead. She spat the glove which still dangled from her mouth onto the seat next to the mess which had been her purse.

She managed to merge with the other autos, moved over to the middle lane, and calmed herself enough to glance back at Mary in the backseat.

In all the confusion, she hardly noticed little Mary again bounced her favorite doll playfully in her lap.

A few miles up, Katelin took the offramp which led to famous Lake Shore Drive, which would take them to the Marina Towers. As they rounded a sharp, slick, guard-railed curve, Mary's world changed.

All that had been unfamiliar to the little girl suddenly became familiar. For on this day an adoption was fore-ordained. In a time when there was no such thing as time—or space, for that matter—and in a place of singularity where all of the laws of nature that we think we understand break down like an old watch, a steady Hand had etched the name of a child of light in the clouds of heaven, a child whose ears were not meant to hear the crush of metal on metal.

A life ended and death was destroyed in an instant on an interstate offramp north of a city, for in a kingdom not of this world there is no difference between them. And in fact there is a certain liberty in it all, like a cleansing stream carries away mud from an open hand. It is a liberty that is sovereignly immune to the groaning voices of sorrow and confusion which arise from the Earth, and that cannot, at times, be comprehended— nor is it meant to be.

21

The Adducing Eye

"WHAT WE ARE HERE to decide, gentlemen," said Judge Alexander, slumping back in his black leather chair, "is if it is prudent to continue under the circumstances." The elderly judge looked first at Will Dysley, then at Randell Clive.

The mood was solemn in Judge Alexander's chamber that morning. There was also an undercurrent of stiffness and discord. This was, after all, the first time Randell Clive and Will Dysley had been literally face to face since their confrontational words at the close of the mock trial in the law school classroom twenty-five years ago. You could almost see the sparks from the opposing electrical fields as they clashed somewhere between the uncomfortable shiftings of the two gentlemen attorneys seated before the judge.

Randell Clive was the first to vocalize his opinion on the matter at hand.

"I don't see how we can continue," he said, "in light of what has happened. I think we've done enough damage."

Will smiled at what he determined to be Clive's pitiful plea to get out from under a certain loss in the trial. Clive caught the tail end of Will's smile but quickly averted his eyes back to the judge.

Judge Alexander held his hand to his forehead as he pondered the dilemma. He looked at Will Dysley, awaiting his opinion as to what course of action he deemed appropriate.

Will's words were far from empathetic to the situation.

"Your Honor," Will began, respectfully nodding at the judge and ignoring Mr. Clive. He stood and began to pace between the bookshelved walls of the judge's chambers. "I think we've come too far in opening the first window into the sacrosanct world of spirituality, a course we all know to be long overdue in the undertaking."

He shoved his hands into his pockets and smiled to himself.

"I've even had it suggested to me recently that God is actually withholding evidence from us like some trump card," he chuckled.

"It was also suggested by this same learned individual," he continued sarcastically, "that God predicted the curious nature of man and provided for us a perfectly rational world: a world which he designed specifically to make perfect sense to us so as not to tip his hand to his existence. And that now he lies in wait, cloaked within the testable natural laws and measurable forces of our world, leaving only scattered missing miracles which are designed to lead the discerning to him through the proverbial back door!"

Will wheeled around and placed his hands on the desk, looking the stately judge straight in the eye.

"Well, I for one am tired of being toyed with!" he shouted arrogantly.

"Toyed with?" asked Judge Alexander, startled. "Explain yourself, Counselor."

"I'm tired of feeling like some lab animal!" Will heard himself say. "I'm weary of the maze and the experiment; I'm tired of looking for the hidden piece of cheese!" Will screamed mordantly, his words ringing like a massive chorus in the chamber and echoing into every fold of the earth.

"A miracle here...an ancient skull there! What's next? How about the thing we all want?

"How about proof!" Will fumed caustically. "How about proof positive!"

Will pointed at the door.

"That woman outside," he said forcefully, "would have no grief at the tragic loss of her child if she had the answer she deserves; the answer we all deserve!"

Will's words intoned of intrinsic truth as if they had sprung up unedited from his innermost soul. If Tom Weber had been there in the judge's chamber, he would have had the answer to his probes the night before in Will's office over a glass of brandy. He would have known this case went far deeper into the fundamental being of

Will Dysley than the superficial rewards promised by victory.

"If she just had the answer this trial brings us one step closer to finding," Will finished.

Judge Alexander looked to Randell Clive for comment.

"It was Miss Magellan's idea to request a mistrial," said Clive, trying not to reveal the intimidation he was feeling in the presence of his old classmate. "What is so important to you, Mr. Dysley, apparently, is not so important to her."

"She is a victim of the same passivity of which we are all guilty, Mr. Clive," Will snapped. "This verdict will be the first crucial step in an awakening of public consciousness until we stand demandingly together and flush out our cowardly creator from his place of hiding."

"My word!" exclaimed Clive, standing abruptly. "Are you listening to yourself, Mr. Dysley? I think you're getting a little too caught up in all this, aren't you? You just called God a coward!"

Will strode back over to Clive and stood toe to toe with him.

"My arguments in the trial have proven that God masked his participation in the alleged resurrection of his son," Will seethed, "an event at the cornerstone of Christianity. He has left us a couple of gossip-spreading celestial talebearers in an empty tomb and a ragtag group of men and women to authenticate the story, to stand on their own merit, which I've shown isn't much. And now this."

"And now what?" Clive asked, darting his gaze between Dysley's eyes.

His expression sickened.

"Oh, no," he breathed disbelievingly. "Are you suggesting that Mary Magellan's death was God's doing? To get us to discontinue the trial?"

"Definitely the act of a coward, wouldn't you agree?" Dysley spat coldly.

"Judge Alexander!" Clive cried, holding his locked stare with his opponent. "Put an end to this madness!"

Judge Alexander leaned forward, placing his elbows on his desk.

"That is enough," he said evenly, "quite enough out of both of you."

The judge motioned for the two attorneys to have a seat. They reluctantly complied.

Alexander toyed with his bifocals on the desk, twisting the earpieces between his fingers. He clenched his jaw as he often did before he passed judgment.

"I'm inclined to agree with Mr. Dysley," he said hesitantly. "I think we've come too far to turn back now. Too many people await the court's decision on this issue; it has become part of people's lives across the globe, gentlemen. The trial has gotten too big for its own good, I'm afraid. It's out of our hands now."

Alexander looked up empathetically at Randell Clive.

"I'm sorry, Mr. Clive," he said, "but you'll have to tell your client that we must continue. Please give her my apologies."

Clive nodded dejectedly, already preoccupied with the task awaiting him in the hallway outside the judge's chambers. It was, after all, his sorrowful duty to tell Elizabeth Magellan that her young daughter will forever be logged into history books as the martyr of the Jesus Trial.

Clive grabbed his briefcase apprehensively and left the room.

Will stood and approached the judge's desk.

"That was a very important decision, your Honor," he said. "You will not regret making it."

Judge Alexander looked up at him.

"Just keep the issues in perspective, Mr. Dysley," he hissed, going back to his paperwork. "Remember what brought us here in the first place; remember what's at stake."

Will hefted his trench coat up around his shoulders as he exited the room into the crowded hallway of the courthouse building. Through the constant stream of people he caught a glimpse of attorney Clive talking quietly with his client, who was dressed in mourning black against the far wall.

Elizabeth Magellan was situated behind Clive, leaning up against the wall facing Will. Clive was giving her the unpleasant news of what had transpired in the judge's chamber.

As Will walked past, he was able to see one of Elizabeth's teary blue eyes just visible to the side of Clive's shoulder. Before he could turn away, he saw her eye shift its focus from looking at Clive to looking at him. It was a small movement, but it immediately caught his attention.

He perceived at first that she had merely recognized him, but then he felt something else. There was something overly familiar about the picture before him. The bustling crowd in the hallway, the garbled voices of the passersby, the colors he saw in his peripheral vision. Had he seen this exact scene before? In a déjà vu, perhaps?

Whatever it was, he felt the thoughts that had filled his head an instant before slip away and be replaced with a single burning desire.

The movement of her eye had caused his world to stop.

All passersby blurred into transparency, all sounds of conversation and clicking heels went mute. Will stopped in his tracks and walked across the hallway to confront the adducing eye.

In his peripheral vision, he thought he saw Clive turning to intercept him, but it was too late. He was locked on his quest. Elizabeth stepped to the side of Mr. Clive to meet his approach.

"Miss Magellan," hollered Will determinedly. "May I have a moment?"

He pushed through the crowd and barged past Mr. Clive to stand face to face with Elizabeth.

"I am truly sorry for your little girl," he said. "It is indeed a tragic loss," he frowned politely.

"Thank you," said Elizabeth, holding back a sob.

"But, I have to ask you," he persisted, feeling as if he couldn't stop himself, "wouldn't you rather just know the truth?" He paused wistfully. "Either way, isn't it just best to know the truth of where she is?"

Will searched her eyes for the answer he expected. What he got was something far different. He noticed a subtle change in the contour of her eyes such that he had to check her mouth for signs of what he thought he was seeing. When he looked down at her mouth, its shape confirmed that he had been right.

She was smiling.

Will looked confoundedly at her.

"Do you know," said Elizabeth, her voice delicate like the harp of an angel, "do you know what Mary said to the teacher who came up to her at the flagpole that morning, Mr. Dysley?"

Elizabeth brightened noticeably. "As long as I live, I will never forget Mary coming home from school that day," she said, smiling fondly.

"I had been called by the principal of the school, so I knew what had happened. And when Mary came home, I knelt down beside her and took off her schoolbag. She was afraid to tell me what had happened because she felt like a bad girl. But she did," Elizabeth sniffled, "after I told her it was all right.

"She told me that the teacher asked why she was standing all alone at the flagpole while the other kids were all playing. And do you know what my little angel said to her?" Elizabeth asked, beaming with pride.

"Mary told the teacher that she wasn't alone at the flagpole," she said, tears of joy beginning to well in her eyes. "She told her that she wasn't alone at all. She told her that Jesus was with her."

Will watched intently as the blue of Elizabeth's eyes clarified and brightened from the cleansing flow of tears. In an instant, her sadness had become joy.

"So you see, Mr. Dysley," she breathed, knotting her brow to hold back a fresh burst of tears, "I know...I already know."

Clive put his arm around her shoulders comfortingly, and escorted her down the hall. He glared menacingly at Will as they passed by.

Will Dysley stood in the midst of chaos and watched as they vanished into the swirling throngs of people, still haunted in some ineffable way by the subtle movement of her eye.

After a while, he regained his resolve and headed for his office to prepare his closing comments for the final day of trial.

22

Chaos and Order

WILL'S DRIVE HOME from the office was one of those drives where you can't recall a single turn you made, but since you ended up at your destination you figure you must have made the right ones, even if your mind had been out of the loop the entire time. Extreme preoccupation is the likely cause of such an experience.

As he pulled up his long, winding driveway, Will thought back frustratingly on the unproductive night he had at the office. He had stayed well into the night alone in the darkness of his office and had accomplished precisely nothing. With the final day of the trial looming up at the next break of dawn, a trial that put him on the verge of his most profound achievement in all his years of law, he found himself void of clear direction for his closing comments. He parked the car around the back and leaned hard against the strong, biting wind as he made his way to the back door of the house, his arms laden with bulging briefcases and his head swimming with the events of the past few days.

The house was silent and dark, but he knew the way. Will walked through the kitchen and down the hall to his study to take another crack at completing his closing comments. Try as he might, he could not shake the image of Elizabeth Magellan in the hallway outside of the judge's chambers. Something about that encounter continued to pilfer his sensibilities; something there was extremely inconsistent.

Will turned the corner and walked into his study. He set down one of the briefcases gently, reached underneath the lamp on his desk, and switched it on. He stood back in horror.

Basically what he witnessed was the definition of utter chaos.

He saw books stacked precariously all over the desk and the floor; he saw empty shelves behind his desk which just that morning had been neatly lined with his treasured volumes. He blinked hard, thinking this perhaps to be some late-night hallucination.

Shocked, he flipped on another lamp on a small table by the door. Again, the light revealed more devastation, more disarray, more piles of his cherished books lying strewn about the floor. He turned to call for his house- keeper to ask what the meaning of this was, but he realized that it was very late, and that she was long gone.

Will viewed his study with mouth agape, his mind racing with imagined causes for the disorder. Was it that his housekeeper had decided to clean his study thoroughly that day and took every book off the shelves and had run out of time to put them back? If so, she would be getting a severe talking-to tomorrow morning. Or perhaps it had been a prowler who had rifled through the room searching for some treasure hidden between the pages of a book? No, Will dismissed the thought; there were no signs of forced entry and—he glanced at a white square on the wall with a flashing red light—the alarm system had not been set off.

This late in the night, with so much on his mind, Will was unable to arrive at the most probable cause of the mess. All he could think about was having to clear for himself a swath on his desk so he could get down to work.

He let his other briefcase drop to the hardwood floor with an angry pop.

Just then, he thought he heard a short rush of breath followed by a quick squeak of leather. He perked his ears in alarm, his muscles stiffened, his heart pounded.

And suddenly, it dawned on him. His state of alert ended.

There was, he guessed, one other potential cause for the discombobulation which had not occurred to him as he probed his list of probabilities. A cause connected with a thought, he now realized, that had subconsciously flashed across his mind earlier as he studied the precariously stacked books. He had noticed a subtle, sort of playful bent to the piles of law volumes, a mischievous lean to the high-rising heaps. And now, coupled with the telltale sounds he had just heard, there was no doubt.

This destruction was the handiwork of a child. A child very much like the one staying in the guest bedroom upstairs. Will pushed aside a stack of books, clearing a path on his desk so that he could see the culprit he knew would be curled guiltily in his soft leather chair.

Sure enough, there, contorted uncomfortably in the chair, was Tyler Hollimon.

Tyler's mouth was wide open such that with his head laid back the way it was over the arm of the chair, Will could see clear to the back of his throat. One of his legs was draped over the other arm of the chair, and the other dangled over the edge of the seat, the red pajama booty elongated so that it nearly touched the floor. Tyler's arms were folded tight to his chest and, Will noticed, he seemed to be clutching something.

Will, wanting an immediate explanation for this mess, jostled the boy.

"Tyler," he said in a half whisper. "Tyler, get up, boy."

Tyler's limp body weathered the brief storm without a warning signal being sent to his brain. He slept on.

"Come on, Tyler," Will said, elevating his voice, "you've got some explaining to do." He looked around the room again in disbelief and growing anger.

Still nothing.

He looked down at the boy and shook his head frustratingly. Then his curiosity overtook him, and he reached for the objects Tyler was clutching so intently, even in sleep. Perhaps, he thought, they might offer a clue as to the meaning of all this.

But when Will tried to pry the objects loose, he got the response he had wanted earlier. Tyler's eyes snapped open. He quickly lifted his head.

"Hey!" he screamed, glaring up at Will.

"All right," said Will, pulling back. "It's just me, Tyler."

Will then watched as gravity seemed to weigh on the muscles in Tyler's young face. His cheeks and jaw plummetted from their taunt positions, his head lolled backward until it rested near to the position it was in a moment ago, his eyes wavered unevenly for a second, then closed.

"Oh no, kid," said Will, forcefully jerking Tyler to an upright position. "I want to know what happened here."

Tyler looked up at Will groggily, and wiped the sleepiness from his eyes. He slowly surveyed the ruins surrounding them, and seemed as perplexed as Will. He shrugged his shoulders puckishly.

"Don't give me that," Will warned. "You did this, boy, and I want to know why."

Tyler gave the room another perusing with slow turns of his head until he came back to where he started, which was himself, and looked down at the objects clenched hard against his chest.

"Oh, yeah!" he said excitedly. "I found it!"

"Found what?" asked Will.

Tyler handed him one of the two books that had been buried in the folds of his pajamas. "What I was looking for," he said delightfully.

Will snatched the book from Tyler's hand. He turned it over. "Where in the...?" he said, astonished. He ran his finger along the book's broken spine and noticed that the glue along the binding had disintegrated, allowing the red-edged pages to separate from the cover.

"It's just like mine," Tyler said as he lifted the other book away from his chest. "Guess they haven't changed much since you were a kid, Mr. D," he said, and had himself a long yawn.

Will marveled intensely at the volume from his past.

A heavy, musty scent wafted up to his nose as he thumbed through the thick book. The clumps of pages fell against the back cover like the deepening sounds of distant thunder growing ever nearer. His searching eyes caught glimpses of words and names as they flashed by. He read: John, Luke, Mark, Matthew, Ezekiel, Isaiah, Psalms, Chronicles, Kings, Judges, Exodus, Genesis.

His thumb caught on a thicker page inside the front cover. He opened to it.

He noticed shallow impressions in the yellowed flap, as if there were once words written there, words that had faded with the passage of time.

Will put the flap under the lamp, his eyes straining to read what had been written there and by his own hand, he assumed, but he couldn't make it out. He remembered an old magician's trick he used to do as a child, and reached for a pencil. He tore off a sheet of paper from a legal pad and laid the paper on top of the flap. He ran the pencil lightly back and forth over the impressions.

His eyes widened in amazement at the words which slowly emerged on the clean sheet of paper.

He felt a tug on his sleeve.

"I'll clean it all up tomorrow," said a small voice. "I'm sorry I made such a mess, but it's always in the last place you look, you know, Mr. D?"

"Yes," said Will distantly, unable to take his eyes off the words on the paper. "It's late, Tyler; way past your bedtime. Let's go upstairs."

Tyler scrambled down out of the chair and took hold of Will's hand. Will set the paper down on his desk and walked Tyler out of the study and into the hallway. The house was quiet except for the empty howls and creaks of the frame as it stood its ground against the relentless wind. When they reached the staircase, Tyler looked longingly up at Will.

"Mr. D," he said, "I think Mom needs double-strength prayers tonight." Tyler then nodded at his room at the top of the steps. "There's plenty of room next to me by the bed."

Before Will could say a word, Tyler sprinted up the stairs and disappeared into the guest room. Will climbed the steps slowly, watching the shifting shapes of the shadows on a square of light cast onto the carpet outside Tyler's room. There was movement in the room, and when Will peered around the corner he saw the result. He saw two pillows laid side by side on the hardwood floor next to the bed. Tyler was already kneeling on one of them, and motioning him over to kneel on the other.

As Will stood in the doorway of the guest room, weary from the long day, he caught a glimpse of his own reflection in the window across the room. The small lamp on the nightstand was illuminating his face from underneath, and the storm window across the room, which was made with double panes of glass for insulation against the harsh midwestern winters, served to diffuse his features. Image was reflected on top of image, only slightly askew, so that his facial features appeared lurid and spectral.

Outside he could hear the wind relentlessly beating against the heavy window in continual, maddening gusts. It was like the wind wanted to get into the room, to smash through the layers of glass and toss the bed linens, to upend the furniture and splatter the wood into shards and splinters, to overthrow and distract with its infuriated insanity. The storm window rattled and shook, but did not give in.

Will looked down at the boy kneeling next to the bed, and his thoughts turned to Samantha in the hospital.

"Make sure your knees are on the pillow, Mr. D," Tyler whispered as Will walked reluctantly to the bed.

His knees creaked as they bent.

"Now you go like this," said Tyler, folding his hands and placing his elbows on the bed. "Mom usually starts, but I'll go for it this time."

Tyler closed his eyes. "Dear Jesus," he prayed, "I'd like my Mom back real soon. Please heal her and let her come home. And thanks for Mr. D, who took care of me . . . ," Tyler opened one eye and looked over at Will, ". . . this is him next to me, Jesus . . . if you can give him a chance, he hasn't done this for awhile."

Tyler nudged Will with his elbow. "You're up," he whispered out of the corner of his mouth. "It's easy, like you're talkin' to a friend."

Outside, the wind seemed to renew its wrath.

From the old oak in the middle of the backyard it chose a limb which had found its dormant winter rest near the house. The wind flung the branch violently against the metal siding; the spiny, frozen wood scratched and slapped against the window, a tangible manifestation of its invisible catalyst.

Will closed his eyes, shutting out the wind.

"Jesus," he said hesitantly, "...Sam...she's a good woman...a good mother...a good friend...and uh... she's been sick for awhile, and...," Will looked over at Tyler, who was concentrating hard. Tyler's hands were clenched together and his eyes were closed tightly. "And we'd like her to come home."

Will felt inside of him a confluence of emotions, like the flowing together of two meandering streams; and for a moment, he was unable to move. Then, with a surge, he pushed himself to his feet.

"Thanks, Mr. D," said Tyler as he hopped up on the bed. Mom's gonna be fine now," he added, and swirled the covers around himself like a protective buffer to the cold wind outside in the darkness.

The first light of the new morning found Will Dysley hunched over his desk in the study. Stacks of books from the night before stood around him on the desk and on the floor as if he sat like a giant in the midst of the towering high rises of a great city. The curtains were drawn open so that he could see the entire backyard, including the ancient oak tree. Gray-white frost ran along the perimeter of the windows, muting and dimming the emerging colors of the cloudless morning.

The first warm rays of the early spring sun threatened the victory of the suppressive wind and cold from the winter past. Soon the thermals would reverse the flow of air and the world would reach outward and upward yet again.

The old oak in the middle of the yard was motionless for the first time in many days.

In front of him was his confirmation Bible, retrieved by the curiosity of a young mind from its wayworn place on a low dusty shelf. The old Bible was pressed open to the flap inside the front cover, a page from a legal pad lay beside it on the desktop.

Will had read the inscription which had all but vanished from the flap: an inscription revealed like magic by the strokes of a pencil. He had read it many times that night and into the new morning. They were words spoken by a Teacher, and written by a child.

The inscription read:

How to get to heaven:

1. Believe in your heart in Jesus Christ,
2. Have faith that God raised him from the dead,
3. And the free gift of eternal life is yours.

Barely readable, the child author had dated and initialed the inscription in the lower right corner of the page. It read, *W.A.D. 1945.*

Will Adam Dysley set his childhood Bible aside and began to pen a new closing statement for the trial.

23

Trial's End

PEOPLE AROUND the globe got up early—or stayed up late, as the case may have been—to watch the final day of the Jesus Trial.

The networks' field staffs had arrived early, tweaking and tuning their equipment so that there would be no screwups. Back at their studios, the network technicians flipped and flopped reels of tapes, making sure they would be ready when they cut away from the live action in the courthouse.

Each network had prepared two highlight tapes set to music, much like they do for the final day of a championship sports series: one tape should the prosecution happen to win the trial, and the other should the victor turn out to be the defense. The tapes replayed blurbs of witness testimony and jury reaction transposed with shots of the stern, penetrating eyes of the two seasoned attorneys and scenes of the emotional responses from the plaintiffs and the defendants. The feeling of the music sank and rose with the appropriate images. They had used grand hymns from a Christian hymnal for the background music in the prosecutor's victory tape; and a powerful, symphonic melody, like in *Rocky,* for the defense's tape. They were even so bold as to use scenes from Mary's funeral in an attempt to really affect the viewer, to touch a chord deep within, and, the producer later admitted, to make a serious run at an Emmy award.

Will Dysley was weary from the searching, contemplative, and sleepless night he had just had. He sat quietly, slumped back in a chair at the table for the defense. No one bothered to ask if he was all right because this look of quiet concentration was not far from the look he always had prior to mercilessly devastating his rivals on the courtroom floor. It appeared as if it was business as usual for the world's most brilliant legal mind.

Randell Clive looked somewhat dismally over at his opponent, wishing things had gone differently in this vengeful courtroom confrontation which he had anticipated for so many years. He was alone at his table because Elizabeth Magellan had justly refused to participate any further in the trial proceedings.

Across the way, the representatives from the Longview Elementary school board chatted cheerfully with Tom Weber and among themselves, preparing to gloat themselves and their little elementary school into the history books.

The other courtroom occupants buzzed with anticipation as they prepared to hear Dysley's summation. They believed his words would spell the official end of the decades-old battle between public displays of religion and constitutionally free people whose only job was to lobby perpetually and in enormous numbers in order to influence and effect legislation which would prohibit others from being able to unfairly influence and affect their lives. And a glorious end it would be, they all thought to themselves.

The citizens of the world fidgeted on their sofas, also unable to wait for the postverdict celebration which was sure to erupt in every city and town following this unparalleled victory in the realm of human rights.

When things had settled down a bit, Judge Alexander mumbled some deep, throaty words which no one understood, then asked the counsel for the defense to get on with it and present his closing comments.

Will Dysley pushed back his chair and stood in compliance with the judge.

"Your Honor, men and women of the jury," he began solemnly. "This morning we come to the close of a most unusual case—a case which has transcended the walls of this courtroom and taken us to the brink of an answer for which man has searched since the dawn of time. We . . . you and I," he continued, "stand at the final gate of a mystery which lies rooted in the very fabric of humanity. And today we must make a decision.

"Are we to accept the unfamiliarity of mystery and miracle, or are we to turn to that which we are most familiar?"

Will walked slowly to the center of the floor.

"In my argument," he said, "I have shown that in the midst of the story of the resurrection of Christ were unmistakable examples of the failures and shortcomings of humanity. We've pointed out the apparent intellectual inferiority of the disciples, who failed to comprehend the hints Christ spoke to them concerning his promise to rise from the tomb, which ultimately leads us to question their credibility as authors of the Gospels.

"We've stirred in the effect of deep emotion on the fragile human psyche and witnessed how the women, who were irrational and blinded with sadness and depression, mistook a simple gardener for an angel and came to emotionally guided conclusions at the wrong tomb on that fateful morning.

"And finally we saw ourselves in the actions of a man at the crux of morality: a man named Joseph of Arimathea, a secret disciple of Christ, who was given the chance of a lifetime to proliferate the spread of Christianity. A man who chose, as we all might have, to give in to a corrupt political impulse and make it impossible for the authorities to find the body of Christ, and, in the same stroke, secure a place in heaven for himself."

Will methodically paced his way over to the jury, looking down at the floor. When he reached the box, he looked up with sad, questioning eyes.

"Aren't we told that the resurrected Christ was supposed to stand in triumph, having borne the entire burden of the failures of humanity in a moment's time on the hill outside Jerusalem?" Will questioned, sounding as if he had been slighted.

"Yet, these commonplace examples of human weakness which we've uncovered in the trial," he continued angrily, "litter the very streets at the foot of his cross and in every corner of our cities today!

"Now I ask you," Will said convictingly, "did he accomplish what he set out to do? Is he truly the Savior he claimed to be? And does this myth mean a thing to you and I today?"

Will shrugged his shoulders as he walked along the railing of the jury box. The network technicians back at the studios hurriedly prepared the highlight tape for the defense, making sure the track of powerful symphonic music was in sync with the images that would soon fill the TV screens of the world. There would be scenes of the American flag waving righteously in the breeze and a candlelit copy of the original Constitution with a feather pen laid across it; there would be scenes from the U.S. mint, where a modernized machine stamped Washington's head on quarters but left out the four words under his chin and conferences of ultrafree men and women determining the feasibility of creating a new system of dating, not wanting to be unfairly influenced by the current Christ-based system now in use. And there would be images of people of various creeds and colors smiling and nodding complacently among themselves, having finally received the answer they felt they have so justly deserved for so many centuries.

Will Dysley turned first to look at the judge, then to the courtroom audience.

"The overwhelming answer to these questions must be . . . ," he paused and looked directly into the nearest camera.

"...yes," he said plainly.

Tom Weber nearly fell out of his chair.

Yes? he thought bewildered.

"Yes?" whispered Dysley's *Legal Entourage* in a low hum, staring blankly at one another.

"Yes?" said Randell Clive out loud as he snapped into reality from the daydream scenes of defeat flashing across his mind.

"Yes!" screamed the network technicians, running for their tape machines.

"Yes?" asked a chorus of voices across the world.

"Yes," repeated Will, as if in answer to the barrage of spoken and unspoken questions.

"Christ is responsible for a transformation in people," he continued, "which man with all his evidence and reason and logic has been unable to duplicate. A transformation which turns the hopeless into the hopeful, which changes the horrible into the acceptable, which renews our minds and leaves us strong in the face of adversity. And it is a strength which is so rare and admired above anything else we may accomplish in our lives."

Will paused for a long moment. Many people in the courtroom wanted to yell out and ask him if he knew what he was doing, not the least of whom was Tom Weber, who wanted to leap from his chair and execute a flying tackle of his obviously deranged partner. But no one could move a muscle, especially Tom Weber, who just seemed to wither away in his seat. They were all, it seemed, undergoing a mild case of shock at what they were hearing.

"The resurrection of Jesus Christ," Will continued, "is just one simple story among billions recorded in the history of the world. One missing body of a man who lived two thousand years ago in a far-off land."

Will shook his head in bemusement.

"How odd that this story," he said, a curious smile spreading across his face, "a story I've shown to be riddled with commonplace examples of the failures of humanity and littered with examples of the weaknesses which characterize the human race, can be the solitary source of our greatest human strengths."

Will looked up at the Judge, who sat high above on his throne.

"And perhaps that alone is proof enough of a risen Christ."

Randell Clive's mouth hung open in utter disbelief.

Will Dysley walked back to his table, faced with the blank stares of all present in the courtroom. He said one more thing before he sat down.

"Your Honor," he said to Judge Alexander, "I will be filing a motion to withdraw."

The courtroom erupted with a deafening clamor. The confused media field staffs swarmed the floor, trying to get to the attorneys for an interview. The media management back at the studios looked dejectedly at one another over having seen such a shining example of human goodness, but then brightened when they realized that they could simply edit it out.

Above the din of the crowd, Will thought he heard the echoing words of the judge saying, "This case is closed!"

24

The Man in the Moon

THE LATE WINTER SKY was filled with stars, and the cold, clear night air offered an unobstructed view of the expanse of the heavens. A gentle, compassionate breeze had replaced the tempest of the weeks past, bringing with it the first hint of spring. The tree under which the man and the boy stood swayed softly in the amicable wind, bowing and straightening its limbs in homage to the extricating force. The contorted, thrashing horses, awakened from their suspension, neighed contentedly in anticipation of their newly budding mounts.

The man searched his mind as he gazed heavenward, the breeze causing his eyes to well with tears. To the man, the infinite futurity beyond held perhaps a million questions, but for now, not one in specific. To the boy, who spun on his heels with his neck careened backward making a pinwheel out of the stars, there was only one question presently on his mind. A question about a man of history he was learning about in his confirmation class.

"Why can't we see Jesus?" asked the boy, stretching his arms out as he whirled around in a tight circle.

The man broke from his contemplative starward gaze to look down at the boy, whose hair had fanned out in a bowl shape away from his head. He smiled at him.

"The Bible you found on the bookshelf in my study," he said, "the one from my childhood. I've been reading it, and I think it holds the answer."

Tyler Hollimon abruptly stopped his spinning and wobbled with dizziness. Will crouched down next to him.

"It says that in the beginning," Will explained, "on the very first day of the world, God created light and divided it from the dark." Will picked up a windblown leaf off the sidewalk and twirled it between his fingers. "And on the second day, he made the stars and the heavens, and on the third day he made the land and the seas."

"Yep," said Tyler proudly. "We learned all that in class."

"And the fourth day," said Will. "What did he make on the fourth day, Tyler?"

Tyler shrugged his shoulders. "The sun and the moon?" he said with uncertainty.

Will patted his head. "That's right, Tyler," he said. "And what do the sun and the moon do for the Earth?"

Tyler scratched his chin and looked up at the three-quarters moon which bathed the land in...

"Light!" he exclaimed. "They give us light!"

"Right again, boy!" Will confirmed—then he frowned at Tyler. "But doesn't it say that God made light on the first day, and that he made the sources of light, the sun and the moon, on the fourth day?"

Tyler plopped down in frustration onto the sidewalk, which was wet from the thawing ground. "Yeah, I remember; it does say that," he said perplexed. "So if he already had light," Tyler reasoned, "why did he waste all that time making the sun and the moon, Mr. D?"

Will let the leaf go into the spring-like breeze. "For us," he said softly and looked up as a thin, wraith-like cloud passed in front of the moon.

Tyler knotted his brow at Will. "Us?" he asked. "Why for us? I don't get it. If God could give us light, why did we need the sun and the moon?"

Will straightened from his crouched position and shoved his hands in his pockets. "I guess he thought we would ask too many questions," he laughed.

Then his face became solemn. "I guess he thought we would ask about the light."

"We would know it was him, huh, Mr. D?"

Will nodded as Tyler stood up next to him.

"But why is that so bad?" he asked, looking up at Will. "Why is it so bad if we know it's him?"

Will paused and looked up again at the sprawling curtain of the heavens. He thought of the wisdom of an old man who had spoken about pyramids and chariots and ancient skulls. He thought about how the old man had warned that we must sheath our knives meant for sacrificial hearts and let drop the heavy square stones from our sweat-covered backs. He had said that we must refuse to shield our eyes from the blinding light making its way across the heavens as we search in vain for a chariot led by rampaging horses and the Reinsman of the Son. He had said that we must hearken well to the ethereal proclamation heralded from the darkness of an empty tomb and resounding across the ages, and that we ought to turn from our backward gaze into hollow sockets of dry bone and look, rather, within ourselves. For a much greater sacrifice is required, Will thought, and no small miracle of our own is demanded.

"God wants each of us in our lifetimes," Will heard himself say, "to see his face in the sun and in the moon, and to feel his breath in the wind." *And,* Will reflected, *to see his Son alive and resurrected from the grave.*

"There!" screamed Tyler, pointing excitedly. "I see him! Look! The man in the moon!"

Will looked down at the boy at his side. He gently patted Tyler on the head and smiled warmly.

"Some of us see him while we are still young," he said, his eyes moist with revelation, "others of us must let God transform us so that we can see."

And Will felt inside of him the end of a great battle.

In the starry sky he envisioned a regal ceremony of indoctrination held in a great stone castle. He witnessed the abdication of a host of temporal rulers and the throning of a new emancipator-King, the resolute, indomitable victor of an internal revolution waged for centuries in the heart of man.

The boy offered a small hand up to the man, and together they walked toward the entrance of The Angel of Mercy Hospital.

"Come on, son," said Will to Tyler. "I've got something I want to ask your mother."

··

For the message of the cross is foolish-
ness to those who are perishing, but to
us who are being saved it is the power
of God.

— 1 Corinthians 1:18

··

Endnotes

1. David Hume, *Enquiry Concerning Human Understanding* (Westport, CT: Greenwood Press, 1980; first published in 1758), chapter X.
2. Philip E. Ross, "Eloquent Remains," *Scientific American* (May 1992), 116.

Publisher's note: A recommended nonfiction book surveying the issues relating to Christ's resurrection is *Who Moved the Stone?* by Frank Morison (Grand Rapids, MI: Zondervan Publishing House).

About the Author

John Vincent Coniglio was born in 1963 in East Chicago, Indiana, and was raised in the Chicago-land area. He now lives in Fullerton, California, where he owns a small mortgage brokerage firm. He is a graduate of the University of Wisconsin in Madison, with a degree in Journalism. A diligent student of God's Word and an archaeology and natural history buff, he enjoys the sports of hunting, fishing, and golfing. In this novel he sought to chronicle the trial eternal we all must face in our hearts and minds and the powerful victory of faith over human reason, which is possible only through the Lord Christ our King.